W9-BXL-698

Large Print Sle
Sleem, Patty, 1948-
Back in time

WITHDRAWN

NEWARK PUBLIC LIBRARY
NEWARK, OHIO

GAYLORD M

BACK IN TIME

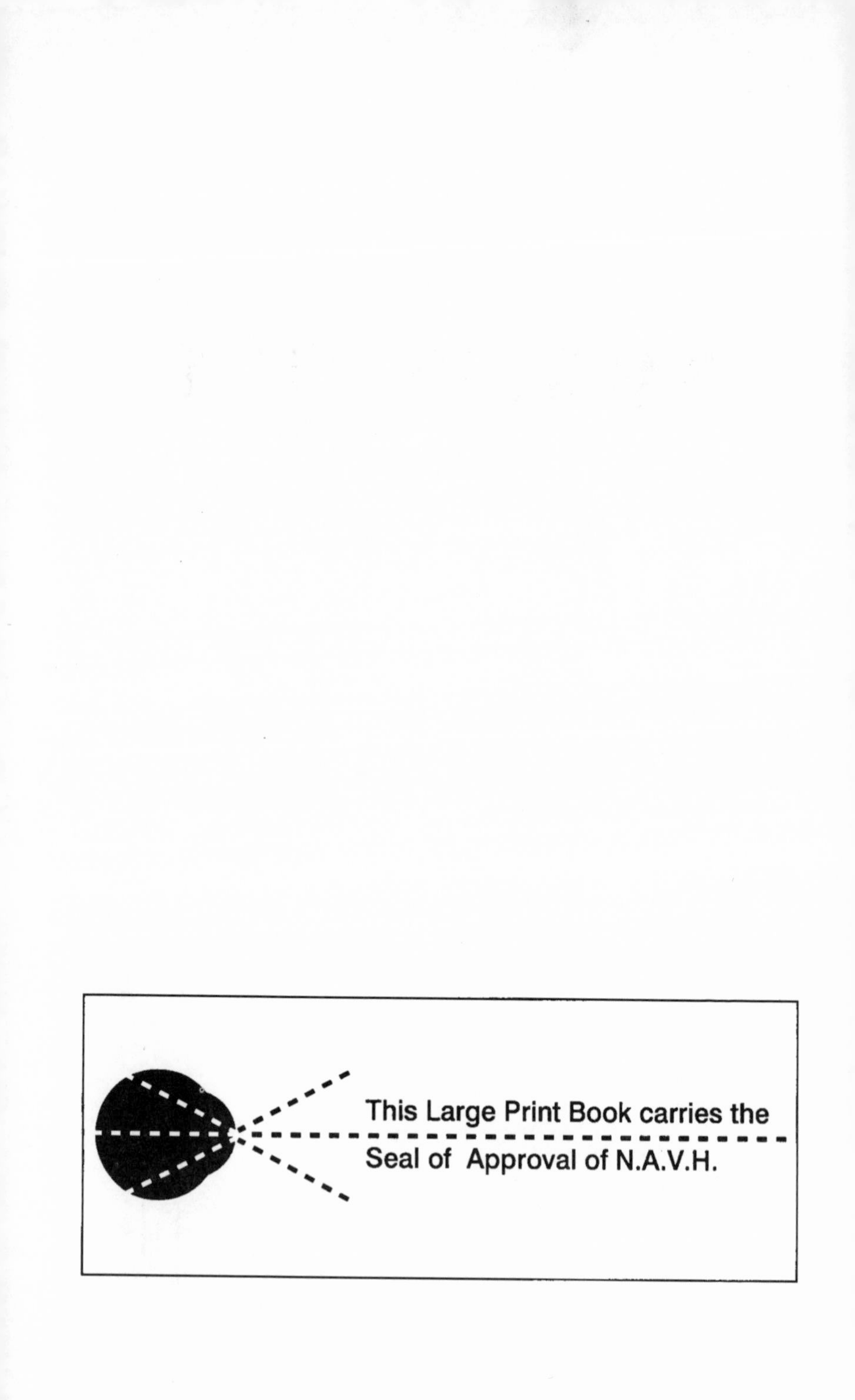
This Large Print Book carries the
Seal of Approval of N.A.V.H.

BACK IN TIME

Patty Sleem

Thorndike Press • Thorndike, Maine

Copyright © 1995 by Patty Sleem

All rights reserved.

This is a work of fiction. Characters and corporations in this novel are either the product of the author's imagination or, if real, used fictitiously without any intent to describe their actual conduct.

Published in 1998 by arrangement with Prep Publishing.

Thorndike Large Print® Christian Mystery Series.

The tree indicium is a trademark of Thorndike Press.

The text of this Large Print edition is unabridged.
Other aspects of the book may vary from the original edition.

Set in 16 pt. Plantin by Al Chase.

Printed in the United States on permanent paper.

Library of Congress Cataloging in Publication Data

Sleem, Patty, 1948–
Back in time / Patty Sleem.
p. cm.
ISBN 0-7862-1567-4 (lg. print : hc : alk. paper)
1. Large type books. 2. Women in the Methodist Church — North Carolina — Fiction. 3. Sexism — Fiction.
I. Title.
[PS3569.L356B33 1998]
813′.54—dc21 98-28343

NEWARK PUBLIC LIBRARY
NEWARK, OHIO 43055-5087

In loving memory of

Louise Jarvis

Large Print Sle
Sleem, Patty, 1948-
Back in time

6485297

THE NEW JOB

Maggie peered into the mirror of her small red compact before glancing at the clock on her desk. Ten minutes until her next appointment.

"Martha," she spoke into her intercom, "please hold all my calls and traffic until after Mrs. Mendoza's appointment."

"I'll see to it, Dr. Dillitz," answered Martha's confident, upbeat Southern drawl.

What a luxury to relax for ten minutes. Reclining in her Williamsburg-blue leather desk chair, Maggie drifted back in time. Had it really been 15 years since she had graduated from the Harvard Business School? What a major shift in direction she'd had in the last twelve and a half years.

Maggie loved her job. It gave her the chance to try to make a real difference in people's lives and to help them live in greater happiness.

Fifteen years ago she had been struggling with the demanding curriculum of the Harvard Business School. Looking back on it now, it seemed more like "boot camp." Like the Army's Ranger School, it seemed as much a two-year management "stress test" as a professional graduate education. The formula approach of the Harvard Business School seemed to involve choosing eight hundred of the best and brightest applicants each year and refining them in the "furnace of affliction," to borrow a phrase from scripture.

The formula seemed to have four essential components. Number 1: Work them hard; in fact, bury them in work. Number 2: Demand a reverent attitude toward the mechanics; punish with a lowered grade any tendency not to attend class regularly or follow The Rules. Number 3: Exert continuous pressure to identify class leaders; penalize the "wall flowers" and non-contributors to class discussion with a lowered grade. Number 4: Flush out the "true grit" of tomorrow's Fortune 500 executives (flunk between 5 percent and 10 percent of the first-year class); reshape the entrepreneurial urge into a corporate caretaker mentality.

Maggie had felt like a round peg in a square hole at "The Business School," as its alumni refer to it. Still, who would have guessed the radical career shift she would go through after graduating with that coveted MBA?

Maybe it was her failed marriage right after graduation that caused her to shift gears.

It made her cringe to imagine what it would be like now if she had made the decision to remain in a violent marriage, especially with a child. Involuntarily, a shudder came over her, and the faces of several women she had counseled came to mind. Battered women. Lonely women. Frightened women. Women so accustomed to explaining and understanding and covering up for their abusers that their whole life had become deceitful and apologetic. They came to Maggie now for counseling, and she tried to help them without letting them know that she had once been where they were now.

The first few times she had counseled abused women she had decided to tell the women that she, too, had been in an abusive relationship. Revealing that fact had proved to be a mistake. The result of that counseling style had been the opposite of her hopes and expectations. Instead of generating confidence in the women, Maggie's confession had only seemed to deepen their despair. Why? Maggie was never quite sure why that was, but it seemed the women were more apt to crawl into their shell when they compared themselves to Maggie — an attractive professional woman who had graduated from Harvard Business School and then Yale Divinity School as a single mom and who had replaced an abusive mate with a loving husband and three children. It seemed to intimidate the women and make them belittle themselves and shrink from that first tiny but important step they needed to make in order to change from victims into functioning human beings.

So she had stopped telling her own story to the victims, and the victims were making better progress in counseling. A theory is only good if it works, and apparently the theory that Maggie's story would promote empathy was not valid in practice. End of theory.

"Dr. Dillitz?" It was Martha again. Her 10:30 consultation was probably here.

"Is that Mrs. Mendoza, Martha?"

"No, m'am, your husband is on line three," replied Martha.

Their conversation was brief and restrained and distant. There had been some tension between them recently, but there was no time now to get into any long conversation before Mrs. Mendoza's session. There had been a wall of icy silence between them lately, but this was no time to thaw it out.

"Do you want me to pick up Ashley and Brent from practice?" Kurt asked abruptly when she picked up line three.

"If you could," Maggie replied. "I'll pick them up from school, though. I'll spend half an hour with them and get homework started and then I'll be back to pick them up and take them to basketball practice at 5:30. But I have that 6:00 meeting about Bible School. So can you pick them up from practice at 6:30?"

"No problem," Kurt replied.

As she put the phone into its receiver, she pondered the distance between them. Theirs was a relationship that had been filled with such intense passion once. Now it felt as cold as marble.

Theirs *had* been two very different lifestyles to merge when they married. Kurt was an eccentric young bachelor given to playing poker for a living, competing in tennis tournaments, and partying with his friends. He'd always been more of a "man's man" than a "ladies' man," although he was a deadly handsome man with a slim build on his 5' 11" frame and a pair of large, liquid eyes that could take on a very penetrating and sexy look on occasion. Maggie, on the other hand, was a single mom struggling to put herself through divinity school while raising Brent when they began dating. With their very different lifestyles, they would never have connected in New Haven if they hadn't previously met at the Harvard Business School.

Kurt's slow, easygoing ways had mellowed her out when she was in divinity school. Divinity school was intense, although in a different way than The Business School. At Harvard the emphasis was on gamesmanship and psychological warfare, with the ultimate goal that the weak would fall by the wayside. At Yale Divinity School, there was a different kind of pressure. It was the pressure to take a "faith walk" while calling into question literally everything that one had been taught in one's life. There seemed to be a philosophy at divinity school that, unless you took all your beliefs one by one and turned them over and shook them and held them up to the light, and then very carefully reconstructed your foundation of faith based on the beliefs that met the stress tests, you would not have a faith firm enough to weather the storms of life, much less guide others spiritually through their storms.

She had "felt the call" to go to divinity school sometime after the failure of her brief and troubled marriage to the Chicago advertising executive she had met and married after graduating from Harvard Business School and going to the windy city to work. Theirs had been a whirlwind, stormy relationship filled with intense arguments that sporadically erupted into physical violence toward Maggie. Usually he'd been drinking, but not always. So why had she married him if there was physical abuse of her before the marriage? It seemed so simple a question.

Now, years later, after counseling other women emerging from abusive relationships, she understood better how some women can get caught up in a vicious cycle of despair. The abusive spouse is smart enough to pick a damaged woman who suffers from low self esteem. In Maggie's case, she had been on the rebound from a broken relationship with her college sweetheart. Sometimes there's no chronic psychological problem within the abused spouse; frequently there's just a situation where one person has been conditioned to give and nurture and the other has been accustomed to taking and bullying. Through counseling, Maggie had come to see that the abused spouses usually have been programmed by their families to accept ridicule and contempt, and excuse-making comes easy to the abused because they feel they really do deserve it. Usually they have been trained to feel that way by the people who raised them. They are often very nice people who are accustomed to being dominated and manipulated and who are inclined to agree with a low opinion of themselves and to take the blame for the insults and punishments heaped upon them in a dysfunctional relationship. Emotional pain and psychological distress have usually been part of love and family relationships for abused spouses, so a dysfunctional marriage or violent relationship can seem strangely "like home" to them.

Maggie had exited the relationship after less than a year, knowing she was two months pregnant with Brent and feeling even more fearful that the storms would escalate and that her baby would be born into a dysfunctional home where he would be damaged. Since the night she had left her first husband, Maggie had never heard from him.

There is another reason women stay in such relationships, Maggie knew. Women often love their spouses very much, and they keep vainly hoping that the problem will disappear or get fixed. Maggie had loved her first husband very much. As she thought back on their brief marriage, she realized, too, that he himself had been a victim because somewhere along the line he had been trained to perform as a spouse the way he behaved toward her. Maggie felt the pain of regret as she looked back on their failed marriage vows and their turbulent time together.

Two years after Maggie left her first husband, Kurt had entered — actually reentered — her life. It had happened very quickly. Having known each other at the Harvard Business School, they had become friends again just three years later. Kurt had been in New Haven playing poker in various card games every night when Maggie ran into him one morning at a cafe having breakfast. She was having a quick cup of coffee before heading to the divinity school for the day, and he was having a hearty breakfast after playing cards all night. Quickly and effortlessly, she and Kurt and her little son Brent rapidly became a family. Emotionally Brent and Kurt had bonded right from the start, and they became a threesome and came to love each other.

Their living together seemed to be accepted and uncontroversial in New Haven. But a newly ordained minister could not expect much of a "charge" if she was bringing her live-in lover and son to a new community. So Kurt and Maggie married just before Maggie's graduation from divinity school. The social and professional pressures of living together had been much more intense for Maggie than for Kurt. A single mom and candidate for ordination living in sin with her lover? There was just too much stress and conflict and hypocrisy built into that live-in arrangement, and it increasingly had made Maggie feel very conflicted as she moved toward graduation.

Kurt had honorable intentions towards Maggie and Brent, but he had felt no burning need to marry, as did Maggie. Marriage probably would have happened a few years later if it had been up to Kurt.

Certain kinds of pressures did evaporate for Maggie when they married. But marriage introduced other pressures as their lives unfolded and co-mingled.

It seemed to Maggie good in theory that, in the Methodist Church, a minister, when ordained, makes a vow to go anywhere the church sends him or her and, in return, the church pledges to always provide a position for the minister.

Maggie's first appointments after divinity school had been in administrative jobs that had been perfect for her child-rearing years. She had lots of maternity leave with Ashley and Jonathan and they had managed to stay in New Haven where she'd done marketing and coordinating work for the Executive Council of Churches. Mercifully she had no traveling in those jobs, so she'd had "the best of both worlds": to be able to be a regular working mom with a very flexible schedule.

Those were considered legitimately good first appointments for a divinity school student and would have been some people's dream jobs: top-level mediating, writing, brainstorming, strategic planning, and communicating. And the work *had* been stimulating. But Maggie had always liked the thrill of being "on the front line," making decisions and implementing ideas. She had been told it was unrealistic to expect to receive a pastoral appointment — especially for a woman in her first job out of divinity school. That's what she had wanted. But she felt very happy that she'd had a chance to enjoy motherhood by falling into jobs that had very flexible hours. What was that old saying? Sometimes the best thing that can happen to us is that we **don't** get what we want. God had seemed to provide for her desire to have babies and have a lifestyle flexible enough to be with them often.

Peering into the mirror at her faint crow's feet, Maggie knew she wouldn't have a church now if it hadn't been for the war as well as the internal furor that had erupted at Golgotha United Methodist Church. She hadn't been sent into Golgotha so much as a minister as a problem-solver and troubleshooter. "Interim minister" was her official charge and it involved controlling and redirecting a church demoralized by world events and tormented by the Middle East war. The church's senior minister had "felt a call" to work with the Salvation Army in its war-related activities, and then the associate minister had received a sudden appointment as a senior minister to a large church in a university town when its pastor died suddenly of AIDS. So without ever having led a church before, suddenly Maggie was acting leader of a 1,500-person congregation.

Maggie had been way down on the list of possible appointees to a senior minister or even associate minister job, but the war had changed all that. More and more of the relief agencies were reaching out to top church administrators as they expanded their war support activities in the Middle East as well as their help to the relatives who had become homeless, impoverished, and displaced by the war.

Church officials really had, on the spur of the moment, no one else to send when the call came out from Golgotha United Methodist Church that its two ministers were leaving.

If it is true that there are extraordinary opportunities that come around randomly in one's life, this opportunity had led to Maggie's appointment to her "dream job." Now that Brent was thirteen and Jonathan nine and Ashley seven, it was time to do something else in life other than manage "think tanks" and public relations and executive decision making. There weren't so many runny noses to wipe now, and their most frequent request of Maggie was "Watch me, Mom" instead of "Hold me." Maggie could turn to more demanding professional activities as long as she could arrange a taxi service for the kids in the afternoon to courier them to and from their activities.

But the hours were excessive in the job just now. For one thing, she was replacing two people. It was not so much a caretaking situation as a firefighting job at this large, Southern church. She found herself ministering to a distraught and anguished body of people suffering at the hands of a remote war that was maiming and murdering so many of the hometown boys as well as the transplants to this town adjacent to the world's largest U.S. military base.

There was one positive result of the war, though. In the midst of the turbulent situation at Golgotha UMC in Greenfield, NC, and in the world, parishioners were willing to suspend their prejudice against women as senior ministers. In Maggie's case, parishioners had been told by the district superintendent that it meant accepting a razor-sharp administrator for only a six- to twelve- month appointment. Parishioners knew when they accepted her that she was untested in the pulpit but, at least by reputation, skilled in writing, managing, and communicating. What could Golgotha lose, since they didn't have any long-term commitment? Some of the congregation probably felt curious about what a Yale-educated minister — male or female — would be like, anyway.

"Mrs. Mendoza is here, Dr. Dillitz," interrupted Martha on the intercom.

"Miz Margaret, I'm so sorry I'm late," gushed Mrs. Mendoza as she burst into the cherry bookcase-lined office where Maggie sat behind her desk.

Maggie walked to the counseling corner of her large rectangular office and reflected on the irony that a person unhappy in her own marriage would be counseling another human being trapped in a loveless relationship. Maggie's own marriage was not so much loveless as lifeless. It was more like a ten-year marriage in need of a spark plug.

Mrs. Mendoza arranged for these therapy sessions every three weeks with "Miz Margaret," as many of Golgotha's church members called her. They found Dr. Dillitz a youthful and upbeat leader during these times of stress. Probably considered by some to be too pretty and curvaceous to be a minister, Maggie was being enthusiastically received as a powerful preacher and well organized administrator after her first few sermons and her first few weeks on the job.

Ten minutes into the counseling session the buzzer sounded on Maggie's desk. *Someone must have died,* Maggie thought. *Martha knows that it is inappropriate to interrupt a scheduled counseling session for anything except an emergency.* She halted Mrs. Mendoza in mid-sentence to excuse herself so she could walk to her desk to answer the buzzer.

"Yes, Martha, what is it?" she asked, holding down the buzzer to hear the urgent message.

Martha's voice sounded flustered and apologetic. "Dr. Dillitz, I'm very sorry to bother you, but there's someone on the phone who absolutely insists on talking with you now. She says she's your mother. I tried to explain that you're in a counseling session, but she's demanding to talk with you immediately."

"Put her through," Maggie replied. She knew Martha wasn't at fault for the breach of etiquette in interrupting the counseling session.

"Well, I thought you might generously decide to spare a few moments to talk with your mother, Maggie," said a distinctly unfriendly voice on the other end of the phone.

"Hello, mother," she answered without emotion in her voice, trying to brace herself for the tirade.

"Your brother's birthday is coming up soon, you know, and I thought you might want to make a sisterly gesture toward him. He hasn't been doing that well. I thought you might come home and try to use some of your fancy counseling techniques on him."

Nothing ever changes where that woman is concerned, Maggie thought. *Always grasping, always demanding, always trying to bully me into doing something for her little boy and my brother and trying to make me feel as though I'm not doing enough in the process.*

"Mother, I'm in the middle of a counseling session right now," Maggie replied.

"Oh, yes, of course, I forgot, you're a big minister now with no time for your family. Well, I don't care about myself, Miss Ph.D., but you ought to have enough concern for your brother to help him celebrate his birthday and show him a little warmth."

"I can't come home for his birthday, mother," Maggie responded. "That's the same weekend as the Harvard Business

School Reunion, and I've made plans to go to Boston."

"Well, that doesn't surprise me, Dr. Dillitz," her mother responded sarcastically. "You never do anything for your family anyway."

Maggie heard the click, and then she put the phone back in its cradle and walked back to Mrs. Mendoza.

"Please continue, I'm sorry," Maggie said, as she sat down and attempted to resume the counseling session. Actually she was only half there for the rest of the counseling session. Her mind was drifting back, wondering if there had ever been an actual moment in time when her mother's resentment of her had started. Not that her mother had ever seemed a particularly happy person. She'd married a man she barely tolerated and then spent her life belittling and criticizing him and making him feel that the best thing he'd ever done was marry her. Maggie was the older of the two children they'd had together. And it was Maggie's misfortune to be smarter and more successful than her baby brother. In Maggie's mother's mind, Maggie's successes only humiliated her baby brother, who never seemed to be able to keep a job, stay in a marriage (he'd had three so far), or stay out of minor skirmishes with the police. Maggie wondered how her brother's failures could be attributed to her, but that's how Maggie's mother saw it. So the only relationship she'd ever had with her mother was one of overbearing hostility and aggressive demands. There was nothing she could ever do to satisfy the woman, Maggie knew that. Still, it made her sad every time she became the misdirected target of her mother's venomous anger and belligerent unhappiness. The only way Maggie eventually had been able to make sense of the senselessness of it all was to assume that her mother must have an undiagnosed mental problem, perhaps some sort of manic depression, that drove her to fits and paranoia. That at least opened up the possibility that her real mother was just buried somewhere underneath all that obnoxious behavior and hateful attitude, unable to escape.

After the counseling session with Mrs. Mendoza, Maggie went to her computer to create Sunday's sermon.

She was excited that the Sermon on the Mount that contained the Beatitudes would be the subject of next Sunday's lesson. That's where her main thrill had been lately — in the writing and sermonizing. Maybe it was the Norman Vincent Peale style of what Maggie said each Sunday but, whatever it was, people all over this Army town were flocking to hear this lady preacher who was getting rave reviews.

The Beatitudes certainly did seem to contain the main principles behind "living right," as Maggie's grandmother would say. Being ***poor in spirit:*** feeling our impoverished state apart from God. Cultivating an attitude of ***mourning:*** really feeling sorry about the acts of sin in the world and for our own personal sins. Being ***meek:*** trying to maintain a state of humility and cheerfulness and gratitude. Having a ***hunger and thirst for righteousness:*** wanting our own lives and the lives of others to be lived in a moral way. Practicing forgiveness and ***mercifulness:*** trying to live life overlooking the worst in others and trying to forgive as God forgives — by *forgetting* the wrong. She'd always liked the way one of her divinity school professors had put it: forgiveness without forgetting, he had said, is like burying the hatchet in the ground with the handle sticking out.

In divinity school Maggie had been intrigued by Dr. Danfield's theory that the features of the Christian character that Jesus described in Matthew 5 were in order of importance. Dr. Danfield had proposed that the "beautiful attitudes" of the Beatitudes were ranked from first to last and marked the stages in the evolution of Christian character.

Next to last was the attitude that Jesus described as ***"purity of heart."*** That was the state monks in monasteries were trying to achieve and maintain. The monks felt that only the "pure heart" would be fit for intimate fellowship with God and for the next and final attitude defining the Christian character.

"Blessed are the peacemakers," Jesus said. Was this the final stage of Christian character development? To do our best to make peace in our personal lives and in our homes and, from there, to make peace in our clubs and in local and state government and in the nation and world? She suddenly recalled one of her favorite Chinese proverbs: yes, she'd have to put that in the sermon: *"If there is righteousness in the heart, there will be beauty in the character. If there is beauty in the character, there will be harmony in the home. If there is harmony in the home, there will be order in the nation. When there is order in the nation, there will be peace in the world."*

It was powerful, that Sermon on the Mount, and Maggie couldn't wait to preach it.

Without warning, Maggie's thoughts refocused on her and Kurt. Maggie was tired and bored with their tepid, passive marriage, but she knew she wasn't going anywhere. Underneath the frigid exterior of their marriage lay a whole network of family and careers and friends intertwined in a way that could never be changed. Staying in the marriage seemed the only way to live this brief life.

But how she yearned for intimacy and passion. And what an irony to be in a vocation which threw her into all kinds of intensely private relationships with people while her own marriage seemed to grow more lifeless.

Looking out the window of her grand office, Maggie suddenly felt ashamed. In the cold light of a winter's day, this emotional barrenness in her marriage seemed a trivial and even self-centered problem. Maggie could intellectualize the problem and reason with herself about it. After all, she had a comfortable and stable marriage. Some people would kill to have what she had — the kids, the husband, the house, the career, the good health. Things weren't so bad. Was it something about human nature that destined it to be perpetually unsatisfied? No matter what we have, to hunger for something else?

Whether the problem was trivial or not,

the stress it produced was definitely real and debilitating. After all, God made Eve to be a companion for Adam. God had verified the need for human touch and emotional contact as one of man's primary needs. The need to be in a state of deep intimacy with another human being seemed blessed and ordained.

It appeared that man's problems in life seemed to arise precisely because people do not always do what God predestined them to do. And the act of creating mutually satisfying intimate relationships appeared to be the hardest thing in life for most people. *"The things I don't want to do, I do; and the things I want to do, I seem unable to do,"* once complained the Apostle Paul. Yes, Paul hit a nerve when he made that remark 20 centuries ago. He put his finger on a timeless problem of the frail and well-intentioned mortal.

Still, it was unsatisfying to have a marriage that seemed like "all business." Perceived as a free-spirited and unique couple by most of their acquaintances and friends, Maggie and Kurt had slowly over the years settled into the demanding routine and busy humdrum of married life with kids and careers. Maybe the passion and emotional intensity just got squashed by the hustle-bustle. No, it hadn't been squashed. It was more like it had been leaking out, without noise or motion, over the years. And that's where Maggie's pain came from. It was painful to feel the spark go out of a relationship. It hurt to look at the process and it hurt to experience the stifled longing for human passion.

Maggie turned out the light in her office. "I'm picking up my kids, Martha. I'll be back at four-thirty. Call me at home if you need me before then."

THE CLASS REUNION

Halfway into the plane ride to Boston, Maggie realized she missed Kurt. She was so used to traveling with him whenever she left home for pleasure. For some reason, no matter how poorly they might be getting along, there was something about being on vacation that always transformed them into carefree, romantic companions again.

But this trip that meant so much to her wasn't possible for him. There was just too much going on with his construction business. With seven homes under construction and only one presold, the pressure was intense to finish and sell the six "spec" houses before the economy got worse. Interest rates were coming down but, in a military town terrorized by a war a continent away, home buying was the last thing on people's minds. Who wanted to buy a house when there was a possibility of the spouse getting killed?

Kurt had been so distracted and preoccupied lately. It might have done him good to get away, but if he'd brought the worry with him, it wouldn't have been a relaxing trip for either of them.

Her fifteenth Business School reunion!

Had it really been fifteen years? Because she'd been back to the fifth and tenth reunions, it felt like she was going to visit a bunch of close friends, especially her seven buddies known as the "Great Aldrich Eight," as they had officially named themselves, borrowing the name of the dormitory where they all lived and where they became close during the first year of "B" school.

Nora spotted Maggie as soon as she walked into the terminal.

"Maggie!" Nora had traded in her curly permed hairdo for a short, soft cut with straight bangs that emphasized her oversized brown eyes.

"Let me help you," Nora insisted, taking Maggie's briefcase. "Where's Kurt?"

"He couldn't get away."

"It must be nice living with a handsome, rich builder. Aren't you afraid to leave him home alone?"

"And how about you, Nora?" Maggie said, gazing appreciatively at her beautiful, well-coiffed friend. "You're the ultimate success story these days. Two kids, a famous mortgage banker for a husband, and your own face getting plastered all over *Fortune* and *Forbes*. Is there anything you haven't done yet?"

"Actually, I haven't had sex with my husband lately," Nora replied with a whimsical smile.

As they waited for her suitcase to circle on the baggage ramp, Maggie expected more quick banter. But Nora's mischievous expression turned melancholy.

"What's up?" Maggie probed.

"Have you heard about Laura?"

"No, I haven't talked to Laura in months, not since before I changed jobs."

"She has cancer. She's dying," Nora said flatly.

"Oh, no, you're kidding," Maggie responded. "But the kids are so young . . . and *she's* so young."

"It's so sad, Maggie. She just found out for sure this week. She's had two mastectomies. Her husband wouldn't let her cancel out on the reunion, though. He's a very nice person, you know. Did you know he graduated from the "B" school two years before us? But Laura is so distraught. I saw her checking into our suite of rooms at the Sheraton just before I left to get you."

Nora had driven to Boston from Connecticut so they raced past the crowd which was hailing taxis and quickly exited from the parking lot in her new sports coupe.

Maggie wanted to ask about their other buddies but any question seemed superficial in light of such somber news.

"What about everybody else? Is Susan coming? Jeanine?"

"Everybody is due to check in today," Nora answered. "And we'll have our traditional pajama party/gossip session tonight. Reunion festivities start tomorrow at six o'clock with a cocktail hour so we can do some shopping in Boston tomorrow if anybody wants to."

The suite of rooms Nora had arranged was perfect: four double-occupancy rooms, all of which opened into a spacious and beautiful living room/kitchen combination.

"I put you in the same room with Laura, Maggie. Laura asked me to," Nora told her.

"Great. I'll just put my bags in there then," said Maggie, stepping into the peach-colored sunlit room and throwing her suitcase on one of the double beds. "It looks like Laura has checked in already."

"Yep, she has," confirmed Nora.

The mood was somber and subdued. It wasn't the same atmosphere of joking around that usually accompanied their get-together.

Without warning, the front door of the suite pushed open and in came Cassie, Laura, and Jeanine followed by Patty, Susan, and Amanda.

"Well, it's about time," scolded Susan as she grabbed Maggie's shoulders and hugged her hard. Then there were hugs all around.

Laura looked beautiful. Whatever sickness was inside her body, it had not touched that fabulous, clear, Irish-pink complexion. Her body looked tight from exercising and her long brown hair was shiny and healthy looking. But her luminous blue eyes looked sad and weary.

"I'm rooming with you, Lady Margaret," Laura said, coming toward her. They hugged and continued holding on to each other in a close embrace, head to head, for what seemed like minutes.

Jeanine broke the silence. "Let's go down to the bar and offer ourselves as living sacrifices to the most handsome men there," she teased.

Maggie smiled. The vivacious, curvaceous, loquacious Jeanine hadn't changed a bit. Why had she never married, Maggie wondered?

Jeanine and Nora went downstairs to have drinks before dinner after they all agreed that their traditional pre-reunion pajama party would begin at eight o'clock. Nora placed the room service order to arrive promptly at eight before she and Jeanine left for the bar.

This "Third Pentannual Pajama Party of the Great Aldrich Eight" had been born from a pajama party that had happened by accident at their first reunion after graduation. None of the husbands and boyfriends belonging to the "Great Aldrich Eight" had been able to come to The Fifth, so the girls had bunked together and a tradition was born. Now, they arranged to come to Boston on Thursday, before reunion festivities began on Friday. Only girls were allowed on Thursday. Husbands or companions would show up on Friday for the informal reunion mixer or for the formal black-tie affair on Saturday.

Cassie, Patty, and Amanda disappeared into their rooms to take baths. Maggie, Susan, and Laura were left in the living part of the suite.

"I'll make us some coffee," Maggie volunteered to Laura and Susan.

"No caffeine goes into this gorgeous body. I think I'll go work out in the mini-gym downstairs and have a sauna," Susan replied.

The kettle began to whistle as Susan banged the door behind her; Maggie and Laura were left alone. Maggie fixed their coffee and then sat in the chair next to the couch where Laura was sitting.

Laura searched Maggie's face. "Did Nora tell you?"

Maggie nodded, and Laura burst into sobs.

"Maggie, I can't stand the thought of leaving my children. I'm so afraid to leave them; they're so young. Fourteen and ten years old, Maggie! Why is this happening to them?"

Maggie put down her cup and went to sit down beside Laura on the couch. She put her arm around Laura's shoulder and brought Laura's face to rest on her shoulder.

"I'm so sad, Maggie. I don't want to feel so lonely and depressed and terrified during the last months of my life. I want the kids to remember me as happy and hopeful. But I feel such despair . . . "

Laura stood up and walked across the room to stand in front of the big picture window. It was dusk. She closed the curtain and then turned back to look at Maggie. She was trying to act composed.

"I want you to do my funeral, Maggie, will you?"

Maggie could hardly control her own tears now. Her voice choked as she tried to reply.

"What does the doctor say? Is there no hope?"

"There is no hope, unless you mean the

kind of hope you preach about, Maggie. There is only death ahead of me now, and I am absorbed by the wildest thoughts all the time. I even find myself picking out suitable women for Jack to remarry. He has been so gentle but all he does lately is just stare at me all the time. I don't even know what he's thinking behind that reserved New England veneer. And I just feel like being held all the time. I have this extraordinary need to just cuddle up with him and hold onto him. I have to tell my kids, Maggie, but I asked Jack if we could hold off telling them for a little while. God, I don't know what I'm going to say to them. I wanted to talk to you about that."

"Do you go to church?" Maggie asked.

"Yes. My minister has been good to me, but I want you to do the funeral, Maggie. Will you promise?"

Maggie nodded slowly and repeatedly, as if in a daze.

Before Maggie could find words to answer, Cassie came into the living room combing wet hair.

"Did you read about Fletcher Hamilton in the reunion booklet?" Cassie asked. Cassie always had a capacity for being oblivious to emotions pouring out of others right in front of her.

"No, I haven't read it yet," Maggie told her.

"Well, it seems our handsome heart throb has changed his sexual preference since graduation. It says in the reunion booklet that he is 'at peace with his AIDS and his homosexuality.' What a shock! You know, he was the *most* heterosexual guy I could imagine in our class. He probably won't be at the reunion if he's dying . . ." Cassie's words trailed off as she apparently realized that she was talking about death in front of a close friend who was herself dying. Cassie skillfully guided the conversation into another area.

"Maggie, what do you think about homosexuals and lesbians? I mean, if two homosexuals or two lesbians come to you and want you to marry them and bless their union, what do you do?"

"Well," Maggie began, taking a deep breath, "that's a hard problem. I can't actually marry them. A minister who is a practicing homosexual can be stripped of his ordination, and it isn't permitted in the Methodist Church for ministers to unite homosexuals in matrimony."

"So what do you do? What do you really think about the gay issue? Is it sin? Or did God make some people that way?"

Maggie took another deep breath and tried to choose her words carefully. "I think I understand the deep longing homosexuals have for intimacy and the need to belong to someone. I feel a deep sympathy myself for the struggle lesbians have to go through, for the struggle they have with their identity. I try to provide compassion and support if they come to me, but I guess I do feel it is probably not God's intended path. I suppose I feel that someone is in a state of brokenness when she is involved in a lesbian relationship, no matter how faithful those lesbians may be to each other."

"You'd better not tell Jeanine what you think about lesbians," Laura interrupted.

"Why?" responded Maggie.

"Rumor has it that one of the Great Aldrich Eight, one of those formerly most desirable and sought-after women on campus, is living in New York with her lady love."

"Jeanine? Jeanine is a lesbian?" It seemed hard to believe. Maggie continued. "Well, I'm not sure that lesbianism is worse than a whole lot of other things. I think that general meanness and backbiting and selfishness may do more damage than the act of loving someone of the same sex. We all sin, of course. And I don't think we're here to pass harsh judgement on others. Jesus said that he didn't come here to judge but to save, so I don't think judging is our job as humans. We have to make the best judgements for ourselves, and leave the judging of others to God. If I'm honest, I have to say that I feel a human being is in a state of disrepair when he has a lover of the same sex, but I do feel personally compassionate toward homosexuals who are in monogamous relationships. Since God is love, it's hard for me to find fault with loving relationships between same-sex adults."

They were listening intently.

"So what's it like being a lady minister, Maggie?" asked Patty. She had finished her bath and joined them in the living room.

"It has some nice things about it. I don't know of another job where you can roll into town and have 200 people open their homes to you. That's nice."

"I don't think our church would want a lady minister," Patty declared.

Maggie smiled at Patty in appreciation. She had always respected Patty's honesty and directness. In that way, Patty hadn't changed at all in fifteen years. Oh, if you looked at her closely you could see the crow's feet, but she still looked like a size six or eight. Married life and raising four kids in a small town had obviously agreed with Patty. She had always been a smart girl in grad school but she was never oriented toward the corporate route. In fact, Maggie flashed back on some of the lectures Patty had given them late at night on the fact that there was a "glass ceiling" that would keep women from rising to the very top jobs in the corporate world. She used to tell them all, in very impassioned late-night speeches after the catalyst of a few beers, that they were all "barking up the wrong tree" if they expected to go the corporate route in hopes of occupying the top job in an organization.

"Remember how they told us on our first day at HBS that we should look to our left, and then to our right, because two out of every three seated together would one day be chief executive officer of a major corporation?" Patty used to remind them in her late-night speeches mimicking the original statement. "Well, forget that, ladies, you may get to vice president of a Fortune 500 company, but you won't be CEO of anything in this century and on this planet," she had lectured them passionately on many occasions.

So it was no surprise when Patty started her own advertising agency somewhere during her childbearing years. "It's like raising five kids instead of four; really, I call it six, if you count my husband," Patty had once told Maggie when she was describing what it was like to start a business and raise her four kids at the same time.

"You're right. Most churches don't want lady ministers," Maggie smiled. "At least they don't think they do. I wouldn't have a church if it weren't for the war. Everything is in such turmoil that the church members didn't have much of a choice when they got me offered to them, and they haven't had time to look me over real carefully. I was sent there less than a year ago as an interim minister, but I may end up staying if the marriage works."

"The marriage?"

"I mean the marriage between me and this Methodist congregation."

Patty continued. "And how's your real marriage? How's that handsome husband of yours?"

"Kurt's great, and so are the kids. We have a housekeeper who's great with the kids so Kurt and I have some flexibility if we want to get out of town. She's staying at the house to ride herd over them this weekend. Kurt's enjoying the building business. He really sort of fell into it. When I had my job with the Executive Council of Churches in

New Haven after divinity school, a parsonage wasn't part of the job, so we decided to build a home. After we drew up some house plans, he decided to manage the construction, and after that he just went into the construction business. He even started seven "spec" houses as soon as we moved to Greenfield, so that's what he's doing this weekend. He doesn't know the agents in town, so he doesn't trust them to move his inventory in this sour market, and he's got two open houses scheduled for this weekend. One isn't quite ready, but it's far enough along to show."

"Isn't that hard for him, starting over again in a new area? I mean," Patty said, "his reputation was already established in New Haven."

"He was actually pretty excited about moving south. He told me one time that being a general contractor would be a pretty good occupation for a minister's husband. We could get moved every three years — at least that's possible, although not likely. Methodist ministers don't want to move as frequently as they used to. It's just not that easy for the spouse to move, and then the kids don't like to move either, and then," Maggie smiled, "the reasons get pretty trivial, like some ministers don't like having to find a new vet for their dog . . . and so on . . ." Maggie smiled again, "But what about you, Patty? What's it like working with your husband every day?"

Patty tossed her straight blond hair and shook her head. "We don't work that closely together anymore, although it is a mom-and-pop business. I mean, we do different things in the business. He does the taxes and the finances, and I'm back and forth between the house and the office. I'm glad I can be there when the kids get home from school. I had a nanny who helped me with the kids from the time Katie was six months old, so that gave me a chance to be a den leader for Kevin and Patrick and to help in all the kids' classrooms while there was still a baby or two at home. Kyle is going to kindergarten this year and I can really see what my grandmother meant when she told me that 'it seems like your kids only sit on your lap for a minute.' They really do grow up fast, and I figured out after we started the business that the most important thing to me is raising my kids. There were a few years when it was hard, and I mean hard physically, just trying to grow the kids and the business at the same time. I was just about single-handedly taking care of the physical needs of four little kids, and then I'd have two or three hours of very mentally demanding work after I finally got them to bed. But now it's a little different. When the office is fully staffed with good people — four good people — I have time to be mostly mommy. I figure I'll have plenty of time to work when they're older, and I'm sure putting four kids through college will put me back to work full-time anyway!"

Maggie cast a glance at Laura as Amanda came out of her bedroom clutching a book.

"How have *you* been doing, Amanda?" Maggie wanted to change the subject since Laura looked so depressed. Studying Laura's face from across the room, Maggie remembered what the shrinks say about depression. Depression is anger turned inward. The shrinks say we are more comfortable getting depressed than getting angry with others, so we vent the anger we feel at others onto ourselves through depression. Freud said that depression is accompanied by extreme diminishing of self-regard, and he said extensive depression is a symptom of internal suffering. Maggie could see on Laura's face a pain that looked like the pain and suffering caused by depression.

Then Maggie realized that the conversation would probably turn again to death. Three years ago, Amanda had lost her husband when she was 38 and he was 43. He had simply dropped dead one sunny afternoon jogging around the track where he used to run daily. He'd had a history of heart problems but nothing had prepared Amanda to see her husband wheeled into the emergency room and pronounced dead 30 minutes later. She had used her MBA to become a prominent hospital administrator and she was working the day he was wheeled in.

"I've become an expert on grieving and the grief process, Maggie, if you ever need any advice in your ministering to people," smiled Amanda.

"What do you mean?" prompted Maggie.

"For the first year after Charles' death, I became an expert griever. I can talk about it in a somewhat detached way now. It's been three long years since he died, and I've been through every stage in the grief process."

"How are you doing now?" Maggie asked, wondering if this topic was painful to Laura. Maybe Amanda didn't know about Laura's terminal cancer.

"I'm OK, and the kids are OK, too. We've had a lot of emotional support from my parents. I don't know what I'd do without their help. At least I'm not into trying to be a professional griever anymore."

"How is that?" Cassie asked.

"Well," Amanda continued, "at first I got caught up in grieving. There's something you can get into after a death that causes you to believe that your love for the deceased is measured by the strength of your sorrow. You can get into thinking that if you truly loved someone, then you should never finish sorrowing. For a long time, I bounced back and forth between exaggerating the grief and feeling guilty."

"Feeling guilty? Why did you feel guilty?" Laura asked.

"Well, Charles and I didn't always have the best relationship in the world. So occasionally I would get hit by the thought that I was sort of relieved to be out of a difficult relationship. That thought never lasted long, though, because life became very difficult logistically after his death. Thank God Sarah was only a year away from getting her driver's license when Charles died. It was crazy for a while trying to get three kids to soccer and ballet and Wednesday church and everything else."

"And how are the kids?" As Cassie asked the question, she motioned for Amanda to come sit beside her on the couch.

"They're doing alright," replied Amanda as she plopped onto the couch. "But they went through a lot of what psychiatrists call 'unsuccessful grieving.' All of us went through a phase where we overidealized their dad. The one you love can become more wonderful in death than he actually was in life, once you're parted. Now we're over some of the extremes we got into, but we're still struggling to really feel like a whole family without him. The grief doesn't just evaporate quickly, that's for sure." Then she looked at Cassie and changed the subject. "But how about you, Cassie?"

Cassie smiled. "I'm just your classic DINK, Amanda — 'double income, no kids,' according to the sociologists."

A natural redhead with blue eyes, Cassie had been one of the beauties in their 800-person graduate school class. She was, at 41, still beautiful. She had the look of a woman who was used to taking good care of herself — pedicured and manicured nails, fresh-cut shoulder-length hair, and wearing a linen/rayon lounging outfit that made her look like a photo in a magazine. There was no way anyone could wear that outfit around kids. It was obvious there were no fingerprints and crayon pictures under the chair rail in Cassie's house.

"I can't imagine having kids myself," continued Cassie, as if reading their minds and anticipating their question. "Matt feels the same way . . . we both have all these yuppie friends who are trying to have it all — the three kids, the big house in the country, and so on. And all it *looks* like they have is a fancy lifestyle they have to support with all their waking hours. We have some friends in New York who don't seem to see their kids much. The parents have stress-out jobs in mortgage banking and consulting and the kids are cared for by three shifts of maids and nannies who seem to come and go constantly."

"Not all families lead that high-powered New York lifestyle," interrupted Laura, as though rising to the defense of motherhood.

"Just about everybody *I* know lives like that," Cassie countered aggressively. "And I don't really think those high-powered executives who live in Connecticut and commute to their jobs in New York have any better lifestyles. At least the mother can stay home and raise the kids, but the father rarely sees them except on weekends. He catches the train before they get up in the morning and arrives home after they've gone to bed. I guess I was raised too traditionally. My dad worked at Sears, and my mom stayed home. I just can't see raising kids in the maniac, yuppie lifestyle that surrounds us. We all think we're so in control, but we're just slaves to capitalism in this world we live in.

At least Matt and I both feel the same way. Oh, we like kids fine but having any ourselves just doesn't seem practical. I do *not* want to raise kids in a frenzied, harried lifestyle with all the intense economic pressures that I see my friends raising theirs in. We moved to Atlanta two years ago mainly to make a major lifestyle change from the hectic northeast, but I still see a lot of stress-out and burnout in the families we know in 'Hotlanta,' too." Maggie gazed affectionately at her friend and thought how little she'd changed in fifteen years. She was still the same bold, opinionated, moral, independent thinker.

The phone rang and Cassie lifted the receiver off the hook in the kitchen.

"It's for you, Maggie."

"I'll pick up in the bedroom; it's probably Kurt."

As Maggie walked toward the bedroom to answer the phone, there were raps on the front door.

"Let us in, or we'll huff and puff and blow your house down," giggled Jeanine and Nora in chorus. Cassie jumped to open the front door and the drunken duo nearly fell into the room. This was *deja vu*. Maggie had a flashback from fifteen years ago of Nora and Jeanine coming into their dormitory suite looking much the same as they did now — inebriated and happy, after spending an evening together in Cambridge hitting the musical night spots and chatting with an army of handsome, intelligent undergrads from Harvard. As soon as they closed the door behind them, it opened again and there stood Serious Susan, wearing a terrycloth bath robe and looking flushed in the face, apparently from the heat of a hot tub. She cast a conspicuously disgusted look at Nora and Jeanine. There again, nothing had changed in 15 years. Their drinking and late-night insobriety had always annoyed the prim-and-proper Susan.

"Is Maggie here?" Jeanine asked, looking at Laura.

"She just walked into the bedroom to catch the phone," replied Laura, pointing to the bedroom door where she saw Maggie holding the receiver to her ear and waving hello.

Now they were all together. Jeanine, Nora, Laura, Susan, Cassie, Amanda, Patty, and Maggie.

"How's Maggie doing anyway?" asked Nora, obviously a little tipsy from the drinking.

"She seems to be doing fine," answered Laura.

"I still can't see Maggie as a minister, can you?" chuckled Nora.

"Why not?" Susan asked.

"For one thing, she's too pretty," declared Nora. "How can you look like Maggie and be an effective minister?"

"What do you mean?" Laura wondered, in a defensive tone of voice.

"She's too curvy and too pretty, I said," repeated Nora. "It's not all that hard to understand. Just look at Maggie objectively and tell me if she looks like a minister to you."

No one said anything at first, as though they were hoping that Nora's alcohol-loosened tongue would just stop wagging voluntarily. Slowly all of them looked around the room at each other, eyes meeting eyes in silent stares that seemed to confess that they all understood that a trademark Nora monologue was in the process of creation and production. Once Nora began, there was no stopping her quickly and easily.

It did seem like old times.

Walking back from the kitchen after pouring Jeanine and herself another beer, Nora deposited herself on the couch beside Amanda.

"Oh, then, forget the way Maggie looks," continued Nora. "She's obviously too sensual to be a minister and you all know exactly what I mean. But put that aside for a moment. Just tell me the truth: Would you have predicted in grad school that Maggie would be a minister one day, even forgetting the fact that no one from the Harvard Business School gives up capitalism for theology?"

They all seemed to be thinking much the same thoughts as they sat in silence, reminiscing. It was certainly true that Maggie had enjoyed the social aspects of graduate school. It was also true that she had never been short of a date or boyfriend during those two years. Mason Tribbles III had been Maggie's scorching hot relationship from her college years, and that relationship had resumed when Maggie entered the Harvard Business School and discovered that Mason was a student at the Harvard Law School, just across the river from the "B" School. A tall, handsome preppy from a prominent New Orleans family, Mason had been determined to marry Maggie when they were in college. They clearly were in love and their relationship seemed headed for the altar except for one thing: Maggie had no intention of marrying too young. Her own parents had married young and were unprepared for the rapid reality of children. They had been teenagers raising children, and Maggie had been consciously determined not to duplicate their pattern. So Maggie and Mason graduated from college and went their separate ways except for intense periods when they would fall back into each other's lives.

Maggie had spoken only occasionally about her childhood and seemed embarrassed and uncomfortable every time she talked about it, and all of them had come to learn that she'd had a childhood filled with sadness and loneliness. Maggie obviously had a poor relationship with her mother. The few times Maggie's mother had come to Boston had been uncomfortable for them both, and the trips had seemed to provide an opportunity for Maggie's mother to introduce her beloved son to Boston and to use Maggie as a tour guide. Looking at that mother-daughter relationship from the outside, the other seven members of the Great Aldrich Eight sensed that Maggie's mother was jealous of her daughter. A beautiful woman, she perceived of herself as a victim in an unhappy marriage with her children as the ultimate trapping and imprisoning devices, and she had vented the hostility she felt towards her lot in life on her daughter while she doted on the only boy in the family, Maggie's baby brother. A domineering and manipulative woman, she was unable to control Maggie as she could her weak and dependent son, and Maggie's independent nature outraged her. Married to a weak man whom she considered disgusting and inferior, she watched her daughter graduate from high school as an honor student, then go on to a happy college career, and then be accepted by the premier graduate school of business in the world. Maggie had told her Aldrich buddies what her mother had said to her when she read the acceptance letter from Harvard: "Just think . . . all those *men* . . . !"

Whatever the root problem in the relationship between Maggie and her mother, it was clear that Maggie never understood the problem. The harder Maggie tried to be the dutiful daughter, making good grades and carving out a promising future, the less loved she felt by her harsh and overbearing mother. And although her father seemed proud of Maggie's accomplishments, in his advancing years he had increasingly yielded to the opinions of his demanding and imperious wife in order to have some semblance of peace at home. Maggie had grown up in a house filled with friction, arguments, and ridicule, and she had been in no hurry to set up house with anyone.

"Remember how we used to call her 'Sad

Eyes' after her mother came to visit her?" recalled Jeanine.

Susan reacted. "Well, seriously now, they say that ministers and psychiatrists and most people in the counseling field end up there because they had such miserable childhoods themselves. Usually they couldn't fix the problems in their own families because they were too young and helpless, so they end up choosing careers that will let them fix problems in other people's lives."

The half-closed door leading to Maggie and Laura's bedroom was pushed open and out came a smiling Maggie, shaking her head in amazement. She was blushing like a school girl and had not overheard their conversation.

"I still don't believe it," she said, shaking her head. "Mason Tribbles is in town and we're going to get together!"

"Uh oh," groaned Cassie, "I feel the heat of some old flames . . ."

BACK IN TIME

Maggie and Mason had agreed to meet for a late dinner after the reunion cocktail party. Some of Maggie's friends at the "B" School would remember Mason as Maggie's boyfriend, so it certainly was not appropriate to invite Mason to the Business School mixer that evening. There was a Spanish saying that seemed appropriate here: *"No hagas cosas buenas que parencen malas.* (*Don't do good things that look bad.*)" Mason was in the category of an old friend now, after all these years, so she certainly didn't want to encourage gossip about a meeting with an old friend that was, in reality, entirely innocent. After dating seriously for a while in college and then breaking up, they had dated seriously again when she was a first-year student at the "B" School and he was second year at Harvard Law. Their relationship had been short-lived, however; for some reason she didn't understand, Mason had abruptly cut their relationship off and, on the rebound, Maggie met, began dating, and married Jake, a Chicago advertising executive, a few months after graduation.

There was nothing wrong with meeting an

old college friend for dinner whom she hadn't seen in years. But if there was nothing wrong, then why did she feel a twinge of guilt, Maggie wondered. As she thought about it, Maggie realized what was causing the feeling that seemed like guilt. It was pure excitement. Mason and Maggie had experienced a powerful, passionate, and tender relationship for two years when they were in college.

It was still a mystery why Mason had withdrawn from the relationship which they had restarted when their paths crossed again in Boston. Maggie had never figured out why he had just "opted out." There was never an explanation, just withdrawal and silence after a telephone call she had made to him in which he had told her he just thought it was "the best way" for them if they didn't remain romantically involved. She could still vividly remember that telephone call and the mechanical coldness in his voice.

"So you don't even care," she had sobbed.

"No, it's not that," he had answered wearily. "I just think it's better this way."

She had not seen him since that telephone conversation over sixteen years ago. It might very well have ended differently with them. Marriage had seemed their clear destination until something in Mason's life or head changed their route. She had tried to guess all these years what made Mason run. Tonight she would ask him directly. One of his best friends had offered Maggie the explanation that Mason just probably thought it would end again, anyway, as it had in college the time before, so he may have made the decision to exit before the passion increased along with the likelihood of rejection and potential for pain. She would ask him directly about that tonight, she vowed. She had to know.

Suddenly Maggie felt fragile and vulnerable at the thought of seeing Mason. Throughout their years of companionship, she had simply taken for granted the fact that they had a deeply satisfying sexual relationship. It was not far into her marriage with Kurt that Maggie realized that a satisfying sexual relationship was not guaranteed in marriage. To Kurt, sex was like a physical itch that had to be scratched quickly on occasion, and his need was infrequent. Kurt wasn't frigid, but he was passive and selfish where sex was concerned. When Maggie and Kurt had sex, it was a brief encounter lasting just long enough for Kurt to achieve some physical relief. Maggie had cried herself to sleep many nights in aching disappointment over their sexual life. On a few long car trips she had tried to explain her frustration and disappointment to him, but it was hard to explain a longing for deep intimacy to someone who clearly did not feel the need. And it always seemed like a sad conversation to have with someone, anyway, because it felt pointless to have to beg for intimacy.

Kurt always had an explanation: he was too tired, or he was distracted by some business problem, or he was upset with some aspect of her behavior toward him that day — but the ache Maggie felt was made more hurtful because she knew that there was simply an absence of desire on his part. Not to be wanted by Kurt as Mason had wanted her, or as other men had wanted her, was completely disorienting to her as a woman. Her sex life with her husband had been a bitter disappointment, and she had come to realize that communication doesn't solve all problems in a marriage. Although the lack of a satisfactory sex life had long been an issue between Kurt and Maggie, the dysfunction lay buried under the layers of duty and responsibility and family relationships that glued them together.

The thought of seeing Mason later tonight made Maggie tremble with a feeling that felt like fear and delight combined.

"Hi, Maggie," yelled a slim brunette as

Maggie entered the Radisson ballroom where the cocktail party was in full swing.

It was Barbara from section B. She and Maggie had been friends by the end of the second year at business school, but they had not corresponded since graduation. Within a moment of their meeting, Barbara was emptying herself to Maggie. Maggie was prepared for it and accustomed to it. It seemed to be an occupational hazard. Just as doctors got their brains picked about body ailments and stockbrokers got asked for tips about hot companies, ministers always got nabbed at social occasions by those seeking a little counseling or "food for the soul."

"Maggie, I should have made a turn somewhere," lamented Barbara. "I want what you have, I think — a family and a husband. But I've always let career get in the way. Oh, my life is interesting. I'm head of the Management of Information Services faculty at Georgetown, but I still regret trying to have a 'commuter relationship' with Mark. We were married for five years, living geographically apart except on weekends, but the stresses and strains of living apart finally took their toll and we split up. We just didn't realize how much work it takes to have a long-term, committed, intimate relationship. And then I did it again! I met Victor and we lived together until I had an opportunity I couldn't pass up to write a book with some B school faculty. Victor's now in Australia and isn't sure he wants to marry and have children. Maggie, I'm a casualty of the first generation of women to be told we could have it all, and that there would always be time to have a family later on. I still dream of it, but I'm afraid in my heart that I'm getting too old for a few of these dreams." She paused, then continued, her eyes searching Maggie's. "It really isn't easy to combine everything, is it?"

An arm suddenly dragged Maggie from her huddle with Barbara just as a buddy from Barbara's section pulled Barbara toward a circle of people whom Maggie recognized but didn't know.

"Oh, Maggie, it's great to see you," gushed a salt-and-pepper haired gentleman with a courtly manner. Maggie turned around to see John from Section E. John Robert Garvey III. John was ebullient. "Maggie, you do look wonderful," he said again. "Hey, I think you know my wife Connie," he said, pulling an attractive, petite brunette closer to him. "Maggie, I remember we were talking five years ago about the struggle to balance careers and family life. Luckily, Connie has the luxury of working part-time, but I have to leave the family frequently to travel on business, and when I travel I miss seeing our daughters grow up. My children sing 'no more trips' when I leave town, so I wonder . . . what *is* the right balance between family and career? Do you think we can set up organizations that let some people maximize income while others trade income for family life?"

As usual, what John Garvey had to say was not easily assimilated. In fact, his comments overall reminded Maggie that her schoolmates at the Harvard Business School had been the brightest bunch of people she'd ever known — intimidatingly so, on many occasions.

Maggie was prevented from making a response to John and Connie by the aggressive outreach of a strong arm turning her around.

"You're a sight for sore eyes," enthused an attractive, muscular, fortyish lad who smelled of exotic men's cologne. His penetrating dark eyes presided over a long nose and full lips, and his oval face was defined by a fresh haircut that looked more etched than crafted with a razor. It was Buster.

"Hi, old friend, where's Annette?" Maggie responded with a warm hug.

"She couldn't make it this time," he replied. "Her sister is finally getting married and the wedding is just a few days away, so she felt committed to stay there. I'm glad I came, though. I'm really enjoying seeing old friends. You can tell that a lot of people are wealthy now, but I'm impressed by the fact that they're not flaunting it. At least," he smiled, "not too many of them are."

"And what have you been up to, Buster?" Without further nudging, Buster began a long rambling discourse about his life since graduation. He'd joined a major bank and was promoted rapidly, as Harvard Business School grads expect to be, then was wooed away by a computer company in southern California. Again, he'd climbed the corporate ladder and earned rapid promotion.

"Now I've changed companies again, Maggie," he continued. "Thank God Annette and I have had a successful twelve-year marriage. She's able to stay home and be a full-time mommy to the kids while I travel extensively, since most of the company's holdings are outside the U.S. I am more and more coming to believe that there's no loyalty in big companies, Maggie. You know, when I graduated I thought that working for a company would be like having a satisfying and very personal kind of relationship filled with loyalty and good will. What I've found, though, is that there really is no loyalty in business. Business is just business, Maggie. You enter into a contract where you sell your labor for a price, and the company buys you wholesale and sells you retail. There is definitely nothing like loyalty in a relationship like that . . ."

"Maggie, I'm so glad to see you," gushed a tall, lanky, smiling gentleman with a ruddy complexion and British accent. He and Buster shook hands and exchanged pleasantries briefly before Buster grabbed the hand of another classmate and meandered off to talk with a tall woman Maggie didn't know. Maggie turned her attention to Mark.

"What's been happening in the U.K., Mark?" This enthusiastic, down-to-earth Brit had always been a favorite of Maggie's.

"Work-wise, everything's going great," he boomed. "I bought a company in a sweat-equity arrangement nearly five years ago and we've expanded into several international markets. On the personal front, Margo and I have suffered a bit." He lowered his voice. "She had a few miscarriages before her full-term pregnancy last year and then we lost the baby as a stillbirth. She's a bit depressed but we're going to try one more time, even though the doctors are warning us that we probably shouldn't. It's interesting how business problems suddenly come into perspective when you face the prospect of never being able to have a child."

Maggie had encountered the sorrow he felt on many occasions during her counseling sessions. She had found several scripture verses that she felt were helpful to grieving parents, but all she could think of at the moment was Hannah praying for a child after years of barrenness and the priest Eli who asked God to send her and her husband Elkanah a child. The miracle baby Samuel was born to Hannah, and Hannah kept her vow to have him study the priesthood. He eventually took over as chief priest from Eli because Eli's sons were corrupt and irresponsible, and it was Samuel whom God used later to anoint Saul as King of Israel and then to anoint David as King when God became displeased with Saul's arrogance and disobedience.

"I'm sorry to hear that," Maggie finally managed to say. "This may be of small comfort," Maggie continued, "but there are scriptures that can help you heal. The Old Testament prophet Nathum says that 'the Lord is a stronghold in the day of trouble' and I think you can find solace and help in God."

Angry eyes flashed back at Maggie. Mark cleared his throat and spoke slowly, as though he were choosing his words carefully.

"Tell me this, Maggie, since you're a spokesperson for God now," he asked in a voice that clearly revealed a kind of hostile sorrow, "why did God let it happen in the first place? If He's in control, why did God permit such a tragedy and such suffering as ours? Margo is nearly inconsolable and I am really in not much better shape. I *seem* in better shape than she is because I feel I have to 'be the heavy' and play the strong guy in our real-life tragedy. But why did God allow it anyway?"

Maggie took a deep breath. Whatever she said would sound like preaching, but he was asking for her opinion. At times, it really was a burden being a minister. People expected you to have the answers but they usually wanted to challenge the solutions you provided. Being used as a "Mother Confessor" was draining, and most social occasions tended to "turn heavy" for her because people wanted to share their rage or problems. She took another deep breath and responded.

"Well, I understand your grief, and I understand your questioning God, but I can tell you that God does not cause that kind of suffering. In fact, He grieves over our pain. That's what the prophet Hosea talks about in his Old Testament book. Hosea was picked by God to tell the world about the strength of divine love and he said that God suffers when we suffer. God fashioned a world in which He gave man free choice, but when Adam and Eve used their freedom to disobey God, sin was born into the world with rebellion and disobedience as its parents. There's an old Spanish saying I like that quotes God as saying to man: 'Take what you want, and pay for it.' God had created a perfect environment in which there was no suffering or sin or shame, but there was freedom. Adam and Eve chose rebellion and their decision was the parent of suffering."

Mark was listening, so she continued. "Don't forget even Jesus suffered. 'They hated me without a cause,' Jesus said, and even God's only son — sent to earth to tell us that God loves us — experienced the pain of the human experience. On the cross he cried out, 'My God, my God, why have you forsaken me?' I can only tell you that I have seen many people of faith who feel that if we sow the seeds of faith during the good times, we will have the fruits of faith to harvest in the bad times. Someone who lost his wife in a tragic car accident told me this at her funeral: He said, 'After Norma's death, I had a choice to make. I could either blame God for what happened, and shake my fist at Him. Or I could fall into His loving arms and allow Him to love me through it.' I've seen that man, Mark, since his wife's funeral, and he has not allowed his sorrow to turn into bitterness. Suffering is not a matter of choice. We *will* suffer in this life. It is a part of the human condition. But how we deal with suffering *is* a matter of choice. I have always loved what the Apostle Paul says in Philippians: 'I have learned how to be content in whatever state I'm in. I've learned how to handle the bad times, and I've learned how to handle times of abundance. In any and all circumstances, I have learned the secret of facing plenty and hunger, abundance and want. I can do all things in Him who strengthens me.' " Maggie paused. "I don't know what else to tell you, except that I personally grieve for your loss, too. I'm sure there's no greater sorrow than the anguish of losing a child."

"Is this a private conversation? I don't want to intrude," said a voice behind her. Maggie turned to see the face of the voice. It was their section mate Curtis with his distinctive German accent. His voice was the same but he had added some grey hair and a moustache since Maggie had last seen him.

Curtis immediately began an "I-told-you-so" tirade accusing American companies and workers of being lazy and greedy and thereby causing the slump in productivity in America that had led to recent job losses and corporate cutbacks. Curtis had been in London and then in Germany since leaving the "B" school and he had observed, he lectured them, continuing declines in the business savvy of the U.S. He predicted deeper reductions in the work force and continuing shrinkage of corporate America into the 21st century.

Maggie and Mark stole a glance at each other. When their eyes connected briefly they both smiled. Same old Curtis. Still lecturing anyone who would listen about the ills and ailments of American business. Maggie could recall clearly the numerous times in class when he went off on a tangent railing against the excesses, stagnations, and short-sightedness of the executives in the drivers' seats of corporate America.

Maggie looked down at her watch. She had just forty-five minutes to get downtown to the Parker House. But she was only fifteen minutes away, so she could stay at the cocktail party another thirty minutes without being late for Mason. The ten o'clock dinner they'd arranged was on the late side, but that gave him time to conclude his business and let Maggie socialize with these brainy, successful, and generally happy colleagues with whom she'd spent two years in one of the most intensely competitive academic environments in the world. It was nice to be reuniting with these self-confident, mostly affluent and powerful business leaders who had once been a homogeneous group of unassuming, bespectacled graduate students fixated on the not-so-lofty goal of simply graduating from that intimidating institution. They were an interesting group now because, in their early forties, they were either in charge or beginning to be placed in charge of America's businesses, financial institutions, and profit-making entities.

The next twenty-five minutes were filled with brief conversations with many people she'd known as well as some she hadn't.

She enjoyed bumping into Sullivan and his wife Nan. Although Sullivan had been in a wheelchair since a car accident in his teenage years, he never let the chair define him. He and Maggie had not been in the same section so they hadn't seen each other daily, but they had become friends during their first year after running into each other at the pub, library, and cafeteria. Sullivan had been among the most self-assured of the first-year rookies. Here he was, fifteen years later, with a gorgeous, thin, blond, curvy wife and an even bigger smile on his ruggedly handsome face. He was "more or less retired," he said, from the second computer company he'd set up since graduating from HBS. He was probably the most successful and low-key entrepreneur in the class.

All of a sudden, conversations in the room were interrupted by an announcement that deceased members of the class would be remembered with a brief roll call of their names. There were fifteen classmates deceased and one was from Maggie's section. Frank Houser had died of AIDS only three years ago. A plump, baby-faced Southerner with a flair for the dramatic, Frank had always been at the center of the action at every section party.

"There are people," the announcer was saying, "who clearly should have been born in another era. Frank Houser was one of those. He was a self-taught expert on the culture and customs of America in the 1930s, and he was a familiar soapbox to many of us in the class who heard his 'mini-speeches' quoting famous Southern writers since the 30s. Many of us know that William Faulkner and Truman Capote were his favorites, and he regaled us with their literary soliloquies as well as stories of his own life as a boy in Tennessee."

The announcer went on to name and give a brief portrait of other deceased members of the class, but Maggie continued thinking about Frank. He lived in New York after graduation but Maggie never knew he was homosexual until she heard from classmates that he had died of AIDS. He died on life support systems, still in New York and still quoting Capote and Faulkner, less than a year after his AIDS became common knowledge. She felt a twinge of guilt that she'd never called him after she learned of his illness. The Harvard Business School *Bulletin* published quarterly had contained tasteful references to his increasing disability and to his desire to hear from classmates by telephone, but the *Bulletin* had delicately avoided mentioning AIDS.

Why do we analyze and scrutinize so intensely our good deeds before we do them, Maggie wondered. Why do we so impulsively act on the anger and lust and "bad vibrations" we feel but we have to "study to death" the gestures of love and kindness we are stirred to undertake? Like the Apostle Paul said in Romans 7: "I do not understand my own actions. For I do not do what I want, but I do the very thing I hate . . . I can will what is right, but I cannot do it. For I do not do the good I want, but the evil I do not want is what I do. Now if I do what I do not want, it is no longer I that do it, but sin that dwells in me. So I find it to be a law that when I want to do right, evil lies close at hand. For I delight in the law of God, in my inmost self, but I see in my members another law at war with the law of my mind and making me a captive to the law of sin which dwells in my members. Wretched man that I am!"

A bear hug from behind jolted Maggie from her train of thought. She turned to see the brawny frame and smiling bearded face of a long-lost friend. It was Sam. Sam was the only person from Maggie's hometown to attend HBS during the same two years she was there. In high school, they had been only acquaintances. LaFayette High School was one of the largest high schools in the state and their senior class had graduated nearly 500 students. Maggie had been active in student government and Scottish Dancers while Sam had made himself well known throughout the state as a champion debater on the forensics team. His major "claim to fame" had been his defense of agnosticism and his skillful rebuttal of advocates for God and Christianity.

"I read in the Reunion Profile book about your entering the ministry after HBS, Maggie! I hadn't realized that." He hadn't changed much. The beard had some grey now; his hair on the top was thinner now; and, as always, his factual statements sounded like questions. Maggie hugged him back warmly. She was truly glad to see him. He was a long root back into the past in this garden of friends and acquaintances where the roots were many but more shallow.

"And you're still in government, Sam?" she responded.

"In a way. I am still in government," he rejoined, "but I had to put more food on the table so I moved out of city management and started my own consulting business four years ago. Our firm has grown rapidly and we now have almost fifty people in five cities. We're teaching city governments how to manage better and we're beginning to specialize in the area of waste management and recycling. But what about you, Maggie? It threw me for a loop to find out that one of the sexiest ladies I know is a minister. I mean, what's the world coming to?" Then his smile faded and his voice became serious. "Just tell me, Maggie, why do people feel they need some central and invisible authority figure to motivate them by guilt and shame into leading decent lives? I don't have an objection to God. In fact, I think the concept of God is great for crowd control down here on earth, but religion seems to do its job by making people feel guilty. Guilt and shame are not useful as a way of life. Guilt just makes everything harder."

Maggie didn't know where to start. As usual, one could nearly write a book in response to a typical Sam question, and they would no doubt be interrupted soon anyway.

"Well," Maggie began, "this God of ours wants *love* to be our aim and primary motivation. But if guilt and shame creep into our lives, that's not all bad, Sam. You know, there's a word for people who feel no shame and guilt. It's called sociopath. Perhaps we need to feel grateful if guilt makes things like murder and moral corruption harder."

"I'm sure you make a stunning debater for your God, Maggie," he said, looking at her admiringly. "In a way, I envy your ability to believe in something for which there is no evidence." There was a trace of hunger and yearning in his usually ebullient, self-assured voice.

"We used to debate that subject at Yale Divinity School," Maggie replied. "You would have liked the divinity school, Sam. It was not at all what I expected. Just like the business school tried to put us through hell the first month just to make us humble and receptive to their teachings, divinity school was a place where you were encouraged to question and confront and contradict every belief that had been instilled in you from birth. You had to turn yourself inside out and upside down and shake everything loose and examine all of it with suspicion — everything your parents or grandparents ever taught you, everything your church ever taught you. I guess they figured that a lot of things will get shaken loose during the course of being a minister, so they wanted divinity school to be first a place of tearing down and then a place for building and securing. We often talked about the fact that 'Faith is a gift from God,' as the scriptures say. But then Jesus says in Matthew 7: 'For every one who asks receives, and he who seeks finds, and to him who knocks the door will be opened.' "

He remained silent, still looking at her with eyes that looked like searchlights.

"It's odd, Sam," she continued, "but I've always thought of you whenever I think of what Mahatma Gandhi once said. 'God is truth, light, and life. He is love. He is the supreme good. But He is no God who merely satisfies the intellect. God to be God must rule the heart and transform it.' "

The voice of the announcer interrupted with a reminder that Saturday's lecture series in Burden Hall would start at 7:30 A.M. and the black tie dinner that night would begin at eight o'clock.

"Do you have dinner plans, Maggie?"

"I do, Sam. I'm going to dinner with an old friend. But I'd love to sit at the same table tomorrow evening if we can. Let's look for each other."

Maggie checked her watch. It was time to freshen up and grab a taxi to meet Mason.

The cocktail party had another forty-five minutes to go but many people had already drifted off in small groups to have dinner or hit the hot spots in downtown Boston. As she headed toward the elevator, she bumped into a handsome man whose face she recalled but whose name she couldn't place. He remembered her, though, by name, and introduced himself. They struck up a conversation in the elevator. Nate told her he'd just left McKinsey after fifteen years with "The Firm," as the premier consulting company in the world was known to insiders.

"The only regret I have about spending fifteen years there is that my kids grew up and I never knew it. You have to be a zealot to be successful there."

Once they were outside the hotel, he waved goodbye and she watched him walk off into the Boston darkness. Maggie knew the Parker House had a fancy ladies' room so she hailed a taxi. In the short ride over, she located her "war paint," as Kurt referred to her makeup, and the hairbrush she would use to freshen up.

The ladies' room was a sweet-smelling, beautifully decorated sitting room that looked more like a private parlour than a public facility. But then, this was the Parker House, where the tab for two for dinner, without drinks, would rarely be under one hundred dollars.

After visiting the lavatory, Maggie began to study her makeup as she washed her hands with one of the many elegant soaps provided for the Parker House's upscale clients. She took her hair out of the barrette that had been holding it tightly at the back of her neck. Now it fell around her shoulders. The blunt, shoulder-length haircut with tapered bangs was becoming to her reddish-blond hair and accentuated her large, expressive green eyes and jutting cheekbones. She dabbed at the circles under her huge eyes and made them practically disappear with some concealer and blush. A coral lipstick, close to a strawberry red, then made her lips look wet and luscious.

A quick glance at her torso revealed a body that hadn't changed a lot in fifteen years. She was still slim. She had changed from the very thin size four or size six she had been in college to her current size eight. But everything over the years had seemed to grow in proportion so that she had become a muscular-looking and vivacious size eight with a 5' 6" frame that looked almost frumpy and "cheesecakey" if she wore anything that fitted snugly. It was probably her small waist that emphasized her other dimensions and made her breasts appear larger and her hips more sensual than they would have seemed on a less curvy frame. Maybe that's what people were referring to when they said, as they frequently did, that she didn't "look like a minister." That statement had irritated her enormously when she first got out of divinity school. She had restrained herself but always felt like asking, "Well, tell me, what exactly *should* a minister look like?" Now, since she was fortyish, the statement didn't seem like "fighting words" anymore. In fact, Maggie felt slightly flattered at the suggestion that she was distinctly feminine and appealing as a woman. What can seem irritating and threatening at age twenty-five can seem trivial and flattering at forty.

The black cocktail dress she wore this evening looked chic but conservative with its jacket, but when she took off the jacket in the Parker House ladies' room, she had to admit that the person looking back at her from the mirror with the spaghetti straps and full bosom and the slim, clinging skirt didn't look like someone who might be preparing a sermon late tonight in her hotel room.

She notified the maitre d' that she was joining Mason Tribbles, and he nodded enthusiastically and took her arm to guide her to the table Mr. Tribbles had reserved. He seemed to be well acquainted with Mason. Perhaps Mason was a regular at the Parker House. The maitre d' seated her at what appeared to be the most private table in the elegant, dimly lit restaurant which was half full with a mixed crowd of parties of eight, businessmen dining alone, and couples enjoying the famous cuisine and luxurious treatment which had made the Parker House a respected name among food connoisseurs worldwide.

As soon as the maitre d' placed Maggie's cloth napkin on her lap, he politely announced that Mr. Tribbles had telephoned to say he'd be fifteen minutes late and to ask the staff to carefully attend to her until he arrived. He flashed Maggie a big smile and vanished after telling her that the flowers on the table had been delivered for her. Maggie noticed that the brilliant bouquet of tulips —

her favorite, as Mason knew — was different from the rose buds in vases sitting on the other tables. Maggie eyed the card and plucked it from the beautiful basket. The message inside read:

MAGGIE, I AM EAGER TO SEE YOU AND GO BACK IN TIME TOGETHER. AS ALWAYS, I AM YOUR DEVOTED MASON.

Maggie was studying the variety of tulips in the bouquet when she felt the temperature in the room change. She looked up to see heads discreetly turning to catch a glimpse of a tall, tanned gentleman striding toward her table. It was Mason. She felt her heart beating faster as he approached the table. Could he really be, at forty-two, even more handsome than when they were lovers? His gait was still the same, though Maggie had never known him to simply walk anywhere. His had always been a confident, take-charge style of locomotion and, even now, he seemed to have sailed into the room like a dignitary on a royal yacht.

She felt like a school girl, not like a mother, wife, professional woman, and clergy member, when she put out her hand for his gentle, warm touch as he arrived at their table with the maitre d' and a waiter following on his heels. She stood up and extended her hand, smiling. Instead of shaking her hand, he took her small hand between his two large, outstretched ones and proceeded to caress her extended fingers and palm. His touch was intimate and sensual.

"Maggie, how can you be more beautiful?" His deep voice hadn't changed, nor had those piercing blue eyes.

The heat of their physical contact grew intense, and Maggie pulled away. He bent closer and, putting his hands on her shoulders, leaned down to kiss her on the cheek. Maggie had turned her face slightly when she pulled her hand away, and as she turned her face back towards his, she was surprised to feel his lips on hers. They both drew back in surprise at the kiss meant for her cheek but planted on her lips. Something flamed when his lips touched hers — it couldn't fairly be called a kiss — just as something had sparked when he held her hand between his. Maggie felt the inner recesses of her body glowing with a warmth she hadn't felt in a long time.

"Maggie, you do look great," he continued, as he held out her chair and then seated himself in the chair across from her.

The waiter appeared with a bottle of wine, and Mason nodded his approval after a quick glance.

"You'll like this wine, Maggie," he said. "I

hope a dry white wine is still your favorite." The waiter hovered around their table as though he was attending royalty until Mason nodded his approval and Maggie's glass was filled. It seemed that an intruder had left when the waiter turned to go.

Maggie looked directly into Mason's smiling, approving eyes and saw him staring at her, studying her features and angles. She saw his eyes wander all over her face, arms, bodice, neck, and hair and then look back up to her face. Then he leaned forward to stare intensely into her eyes.

"Am I being inspected?" She smiled at him, returning his direct stare with her own unblinking gaze.

He shook his head slowly and responded, "You are definitely Grade A approved," and she watched his eyes roaming over her as though feasting on the sight. He did not try to disguise the appetite for her which was so obvious in his meandering eyes.

The electricity between them was high voltage. It was inappropriate but she felt excited as she absorbed the stares of the man who had been her first real lover. He made no effort to restrain the desire for her that was etched on his face and evident in his posture as he lunged toward her, his right elbow on the table so that his chin rested in his hand. His left arm lay flat on the table, thrust toward her plate, and his face was lit up with an adoring smile.

Maggie looked across the table at his impish, boyish face. Feeling the sparks flowing between them was like being back in a time and space where she had once lived. Only in this time and space, there could not be the freedom to act on their romantic feelings. Was that what added excitement to this meeting? It was like looking at forbidden fruit and wanting to taste it.

"How is your career going, Mason?"

He grinned and chuckled, then reached over to give her hand a quick squeeze before he changed his position and reclined back in his chair.

"Yes, let's start with that," he said with a smile. "I like being a corporate lawyer. Our firm really has two specialties — criminal law and maritime law. I've been the lead attorney lately on some fairly visible murder cases. So I'm involved in big-league law, and I like operating in the major leagues." He paused. "I just wish I had the love of my life to share it with."

His verbal boldness surprised her.

"But you were married for a while. I run into mutual friends of ours once in a while, so I've heard what a superstar lawyer you are. I heard that Connie was a nice person. Very pretty, nice figure, from a good family. At least, that's what I heard."

"Yeah, that's true," he said somewhat stiffly and without smiling. "We were married for five long years. No kids. Too bad she didn't like sex much, Maggie." He paused. "You spoiled me, you know," he said with a boyish grin.

Now it definitely felt like they were in a Garden of Eden with something forbidden in the background. It had been such a long time since Maggie had felt wanted sexually. Even though this was just talk, it made her feel feminine and desirable.

Suddenly the maitre d' was at Mason's side thrusting a portable telephone in front of him.

"Excuse me, Maggie," he apologized, and then he engaged in a rather enthusiastic exchange with the caller.

"That was my office bringing me some good news, Maggie. The conflict in the Middle East is ending as we speak, and that's good news for the shipping magnates we represent since they own the shipping lines that transport goods through international waters in that area. We've been helping the Secretary of State negotiate a speedy end to the costly embargo imposed right after the conflict began. This war has cost our clients a bundle. Not only have they lost revenues, but they've had to pay our fees to help speed up the negotiating process."

"Oh," Maggie replied, trying to absorb the news, "that will mean a lot of changes in Greenfield. It's mostly a military town so that's why I happen to be there in the first place. The senior minister joined the war effort, and I got assigned as senior minister of a big church because of the crisis."

"And how are you enjoying *your* career, Maggie?"

She looked him in the eyes as she began. "I think I'm where God wants me to be for right now. They've always assigned me to staff jobs before this, so I'm a real minister with a real church for the first time in my career. I guess the thing I like least about being a minister is having to listen to church members quarreling at church meetings. The meetings actually drive me a little nuts. And the night meetings are a little hard on family life, so Kurt has to pick up the slack and play 'Mr. Mom' and 'Homework Helper' most evenings."

"And how *is* Kurt?" She could detect the cool tone in his voice. As he asked the question, Maggie recalled that Mason and Kurt had met when they were all in graduate school in Boston. Maggie flashed a big smile.

"He's great. He'll love hearing that the conflict is over. It'll make his houses easier to sell. He's had a real tough market lately."

"Yes, that's right, Kurt is a home builder, isn't he?" Maggie could hear the contempt in his voice. That sentiment really wasn't so different from the opinion expressed by a few other people through the years. Most people thought of homebuilding as almost a blue-collar type occupation that you certainly didn't need a fancy education for, much less a Harvard MBA.

"And has he gotten his financial problems straightened out?" Mason asked. Maggie was shocked. How could Mason possibly know that Kurt had been teetering on the brink of bankruptcy at one time?

"How did you know that?" Her tone of voice was demanding.

"The world is a small place when you come right down to it, Maggie. It isn't hard to find out financial information about other people if you have the right contacts and know who to ask. Our shipping magnates are considered the royalty of banking customers, so I can find out whatever I want to know about almost anybody. And I've been keeping up with you since we parted ways."

"It's easy to get into financial trouble in the building business," Maggie replied, feeling a little defensive. Kurt's financial problems *had* been a drain on their marriage, though. Maggie found herself wanting to provide moral support for her husband and his building ventures, but Kurt always wanted to take on more debt than she was comfortable with. Even now, in a new community where he was an unknown, he had persuaded Maggie to go along with his borrowing enough money for seven speculative houses instead of just starting with one. It had not been difficult to borrow the money. In fact, it had been surprisingly easy. Two different banks in Maggie's congregation had been more than willing to make the loan to Kurt not only because Maggie was acting senior minister at Golgotha UMC but also because there was an oversupply of money compared to demand. There had been a major slowdown in economic activity in Greenfield since half its population was off fighting a war on another continent. It was a powerful profession Maggie now found herself in. Many people clearly felt that Maggie had a spiritual, God-given kind of power that could somehow influence what happened to their very souls. So what it boiled down to is that Kurt usually found it easy to persuade bankers to lend him large amounts of construction money once they learned that Kurt's wife had a "hot line" to the creator.

"It's easy to get into trouble in *any* business if you don't know what you're doing," Mason replied. There it was! Now she clearly saw that arrogant, egotistical self-confidence that used to irritate and awe her at the same time when they were dating. How dare he belittle and emasculate Kurt in front of her?

As if sensing her discomfort, Mason changed the subject. "How are your friends from grad school?"

"They're doing fine, except for Laura. She found out she has cancer, and she isn't expected to beat it."

"What? What about the others? Did all of them come?"

"Yes, the Great Aldrich Eight showed up as usual for the 'Girls' Night' that has become our standard Thursday night prelude to every reunion. Some of the husbands will roll in for the Friday night section parties and for the Saturday night class party."

"How's Patty?"

"She may have ended up with the overall best situation of the eight," Maggie replied. "She has four kids. She and her husband live in a small town happily raising them, and she's managed to combine her professional life and motherhood in a neat way. She and her husband run a small advertising agency together. She said she handed her last child over to the school system last year, but she's not in the mid-life crisis I see so many women in because she's been working in their family business. Staying busy seems to be related to mental health and happiness, from what I can tell."

"How about Nora?"

Maggie smiled. "Nora is as you would expect. She's in a high-powered venture capital firm, married to a New York lawyer, and they have two kids, a house in the Hamptons, and at least two shifts of domestic staff who come in to care for and transport the children while they maintain their careers at fever pitch. Motherhood seems to mellow people, and she's softened a bit."

"Did I hear that Amanda lost her husband?"

"Yes," replied Maggie, "he died a few years ago and she's still recovering. It must be hard to be a young widow raising kids alone and dealing with all the loneliness."

"And Jeanine?"

"Jeanine is doing exceptionally well in lots of ways. She's a very successful and very beautiful executive for Liz Claiborne but she hasn't married. She seems to have a life that's filled with friends and pets."

"What's Susan up to?"

"She's doing OK, I guess. At least she's getting better. She married a guy who turned out to be a real jerk. She's a writer, you know, and she married a guy who was Princeton undergrad and Yale Business School. He was a nice guy by all appearances and very talented. But he was lazy. Susan worked hard the whole time they were married in the public relations and advertising firm they started. But he just wouldn't go to work. He used to tell Susan that his biological clock was just different and that he couldn't function effectively until noon or so. So he used to lie around in the bed in the morning while she went to work early and stayed until late. She said he would sit up all night watching television until one or two in the morning, then sleep late, then roll into their office in the early afternoon and proceed to do whatever struck his fancy for a few hours until he left the office to play tennis or racquetball at a downtown club. You met him, I think. He was very smooth and charming and somehow manipulated her for years. He used to tell her that his sports activities in the afternoon were necessary for making business contacts. What Susan told me Thursday night is that 'the spell wore off,' and she'd finally had enough. She said when they'd argue about his going to work, he would scream that he didn't work for her. I don't know why she ever connected with him, he was such a user. But she grew up very needy emotionally. Her family was very dysfunctional and her parents were always involved in extramarital affairs right in front of the children. I think she ended up being the caretaker of her four brothers and the nurturing presence in the family, so she was more or less programmed to take on a dilettante like him. At least she was pretty vulnerable to a smooth talker like him. He was just plain lazy, there's no other way to say it. So eventually love turned to disgust. She said she woke up one morning and realized to her horror that things would never be different and that she couldn't take the mental agony. So she quietly prepared her resume, sent it out to some ad agencies in Los Angeles, and was offered a job fairly quickly. When she told Martin she was leaving the marriage, he protested mostly because she was leaving the business. I'm sure he knew that he was too lazy to keep it going, and in fact the business did close."

"So she's in LA?"

"Yes, and I think she feels a little bitter

that she made such a stupid choice of a marriage partner. Now she's closing in on forty with very little time to find another husband and have a family. I don't think she regrets leaving him. She just feels she wasted her time with him. He really wasn't a grownup. He wasn't from a rich family, but his parents doted on him and he was brought up to believe that his would be a life of privilege and that he never had to do anything except be smart and have good manners. His parents hobnobbed with the rich set so he grew up enjoying all the privileges in life and assuming no responsibilities. He wasn't even close to being ready to get married, even though he was in his thirties, when he and Susan married. He really needed someone to raise him. But she got tired of being his parent."

"Can't people change, Maggie? What if she gave up on him too soon? What happened to the 'for better or worse' part of marriage?"

Maggie looked into his large eyes searching her face for answers. He was serious. Mason had been divorced himself, as had Maggie, and he seemed earnest about the way in which he was asking the question. She nodded her head slowly as she began to respond.

"I guess we've become a nation in which everything is disposable — diapers, jobs, relationships, everything. One of the ministers I respect told me that he thinks the church's main challenge in the twenty-first century will be to try to help people keep the commitments they make. We somehow feel that the commitments we make are not really binding if we decide we don't want to keep our promises."

Mason cocked his head to one side as he flashed his trademark toothy, boyish smile. It was that smile that had first melted her heart years ago. "Maybe the church can help us make better decisions to begin with so that we don't end up being committed to the wrong person or the wrong ideas."

"Good concept," Maggie said, returning his smile. It was so good to see him again, to hear his brain tick, his heart beat, and his mind work. "But what I'm learning about marriage is that every marriage has some problems that need to be worked on and some problems that just never go away. I can see more clearly now, in my second marriage, that it's really a matter of commitment to stay in any marriage. Second marriages don't have a better success rate than first marriages, you know. But, like the scriptures say, 'if you make a vow to the Lord, be sure to keep it.' I just think we don't take our vows and commitments seriously enough.

We usually don't think of the marriage decision as a vow we make to God."

Then she decided to change the subject. "Speaking of decisions," she continued, "I have to ask you this question that I've wanted an answer to for sixteen years." She paused. He was listening intently. "Why did you just stop our relationship? Why, with no warning and no explanation, did you stop calling me or writing me or coming to see me after we had that cryptic telephone conversation when you said it would be 'best' if we didn't see each other anymore?" She paused and then asked again as she stared into his eyes.

"Why?"

He took a deep breath and squirmed in his chair, shaking his head slowly. "Now *that* was one bad decision, Maggie," he replied. "I can't explain it, I just felt like I was going to lose you. We'd already broken up in college once before because you were shy of marriage, and I had no confidence that I could hold onto you. You were up here at the most prestigious business school in the world, no doubt getting ready to get swept off your feet by one of the hundreds of talented young bachelors in the class. Law school was tough for me, and I felt like I had no control, so I just decided that the only thing I could control was when and how it would end. I mean, it might have been stupid, but that's what happened." He paused and then looked her directly in the eyes. "I've had a few regrets about that decision, Maggie," he said, with obvious sadness in his voice.

"So there was no communication, no explanation. You just abandoned me, right?"

"Right," he sighed, glancing down at the table while he fidgeted with his napkin. Then he looked back up at her. "I guess we both have made some mistakes in our youth and, like I said, I've had many regrets about our relationship ending. But unfortunately, it takes a pair of middle-aged eyes to see some things clearly and, by the time you see them, the fertile opportunities are gone." His cocky self-confident banter had transformed into a self-effacing confession. "There's an emptiness in my life, Maggie. In the background there's still a persistent longing for you that seems to grow as I get older and realize that I should have married the companion of my youth and the person that I loved the most in the world. But the opportunity to marry and have many children with you is gone now. It is certainly the main regret of my life."

The waiter appeared with their salads and

then with the main course. When the food began arriving, they resumed their talk of friends and family.

"What's Cassie up to?" Mason was sipping his coffee after the meal when he asked about the seventh of the buddies.

"Cassie is still the beauty she was in grad school. In fact, maybe she's aged differently than some of the others. Cassie hasn't had to cope with the physical demands of working and raising a family. Cassie and Matt are not going to have kids, and it's their choice. They've gotten used to having hobbies and free time, and Cassie says she doesn't want to raise kids in the frenetic way a lot of executive families do. She was always good at analyzing things, and she has analyzed the having-kids decision and concluded that kids are too difficult to introduce into their lives. They moved from New York to Atlanta about three years ago and have made 'Hotlanta' their home."

"Nothing else, sir?" asked the waiter as he presented the check.

A few moments later they were walking out of the restaurant and into the cool night air.

"Same old Boston, eh Maggie? Hardly a day goes by that there isn't a chill in the air at some point, even in the summer." As they stood underneath the restaurant's elegant canopy, Mason moved behind her and began massaging her shoulders with his oversized hands. It was like old times feeling her tired, aching muscles soothed by his giant hands and nimble fingers.

"Taxi, sir?" The doorman was impeccably dressed in the rich burgundy and forest green colors of the hotel's motif.

"Yes, please," he directed the doorman. "Let's go have a quick drink at my hotel, Maggie. Come on, I know it's late, but we may not have this chance again." He massaged her shoulders harder as he spoke. His massages had always tranquilized her and now, too, she felt numbed into moving in whatever direction he was leading her.

The taxi ride to his hotel was a short one. As Maggie moved her long legs outside the vehicle, she noticed her watch. It was nearly midnight. No wonder she felt tired. But at the same time, she felt an uplifting kind of mellowness about being back in the company of the man with whom she'd had the most passionate and intimate relationship of her life. Every tortured secret of her background had been shared with Mason a long time ago when he became her first boyfriend and first true friend. Every sadness, every insecurity, every aspiration, every fear, every desire, Mason knew about. It was so comfortable to be back in the company of just about the only person in the world who knew her "warts and all." No pretenses were needed, no facade was expected, no mask had to be worn.

As soon as she stepped into his hotel suite she felt even more comfortable and kicked her shoes off immediately. She made herself at home in the large living room next to the adjoining bedroom as she reclined in a plush chair and propped her feet up on its ottoman while he fixed their nightcap.

"Is tomato juice or mineral water OK?" he called from the kitchen.

"Perfect," she purred.

"How's Mommy Dearest?" he began, as he sat on the couch near her chair after handing her the tomato juice.

"Oh, she's OK, still the same," Maggie answered defensively, shaking her head.

"Don't tell me she's still as bossy as she used to be. Old age should be mellowing her by now."

"She's the same," she said, not smiling. "Still trying to bully and manipulate me, although she's become a little wary of me since I've become an ordained minister. It's as though she feels I have some kind of power as a minister that she may want to make use of someday. So we have a polite relationship, but I'm the outsider in the family. That's probably the best way for me. I'll always have a sadness inside because of how twisted our family relationships turned out to be, though."

"That's what I don't understand. You've always been the dutiful daughter, but your mother used to pick fights with you all the time over such silly things."

She shrugged her shoulders and looked weary. "I guess that's been a regular occurrence in a lot of families since time began. That's one of the things I like about the Bible, how it tells the truth about families. It doesn't try to sugarcoat the way real life is. Just look at the Isaac and Rebekkah story. The mother favored Jacob, and the father's favorite was Esau. Mothers and fathers shouldn't have favorites in families, but they often do. And in our case, my brother was the favorite. At least my mother preferred him and as he got older, my father just pretty much gave in to whatever she wanted so he could have peace at home. They were always so proud of their son, but when he began getting into more and more trouble as a teenager and adult, they grew bitter. And instead of being proud of me, they seemed to resent my accomplishments. It was as though they thought that I stole my brother's thunder or his birthright."

"Have you ever talked to them about all the hurt and pain in your childhood?"

"No, ours has just solidified into a rather stiff version of a child/parent relationship. My last treasonous act, in their eyes, was when I didn't step in to keep my brother's third marriage together after his wife left him. They expected me to bludgeon my brother and his estranged wife with the scriptures in order to get them back together. I tried to talk to my brother, but he was having an affair and doing cocaine to take his mind off his problems and was completely passive, almost oblivious to the fact that his marriage was disintegrating. His wife didn't want to work things out with me, she wanted to work things out with him. So my attempt at counseling didn't do much. But somehow I became responsible in my mother's eyes for his divorce because I didn't do enough to prevent it. Jonathan had grown up around my parents' adulteries, as you well know, so he wasn't programmed to do marriage faithfully. He hadn't learned to do it that way and didn't think it was important. Of course, my parents don't blame themselves, though, for flaunting their adulteries in his face. They blame me."

"But you didn't learn to do marriage faithfully either, if you grew up in the same house," Mason interjected.

"Well, I suppose that's where free will and free choice come in. The world is a place where parents have taught children to sin, and there is a lot of sin we all learn. But we have a brain and a spirit and a soul in addition to our feelings. And I always knew that I did not want to get by in this life by manipulating and controlling and cheating on people. I just made up my mind to do things a different way and, because of that, I'm the outcast in my family. I remember reading what a famous theologian once said about our decisions: 'We pay a price for everything.' And I have paid a price for my rebellion against my parents. But I had to choose between their way and God's way, and I have to accept the will of my heavenly Father. That makes me less accepted here on earth by my own family, but it's a price I'll pay."

Mason searched her face and then tentatively spoke. "You look amazingly like your mother as you get older, Maggie."

The look Maggie gave him was one of disappointment mixed with resentment. "That's not something I like hearing, especially from you, because I'm sure it must be true. You've known me a long time."

They sat in silence for a moment. Then Maggie spoke.

"I know I have a love-hate relationship with my mother. She still tries to bully and dominate me, and I hate that behavior and our relationship, although I certainly have no hate in my heart for her."

Mason interrupted. "How can she control you now? You're a grown woman. You're a respected pillar of the community." He looked at her in disbelief. Then he said gently, "Maybe you need some professional therapy to try to sort out and finally lay to rest these ghosts from your childhood."

"No," Maggie answered defiantly, "she does still try to dominate and control me. It's not just my imagination or my re-living my childhood anxieties," she replied, with some obvious impatience in her voice.

"You said you have a love-hate relationship with her. Where's the love part of the relationship?"

"Oh, I do love her. Much as I resent her overbearing behavior, I am grateful to her and my dad for taking me to church when I was a little girl. They helped me discover a Saviour whom I could lean on as a rock when I needed to, and I found the true source of love and joy because they led me as a little child to Jesus. That's the greatest thing you can do for a child. I do love my parents. I just can't stand being around them because they're always judging me harshly and trying to use me to bail my brother out of trouble, and they get worse as they get older. They even made tacky and nasty comments about me to my children when the kids visited them for two weeks last summer, so I'm not going to encourage the children's relationship with their grandparents."

Maggie took a deep breath, then continued. "You know that my grandmother was my real mother anyway. I stayed every summer of my life with her until I was eighteen, and my real home was with her. She always loved me, and I felt accepted and cherished and respected in her house. At least I felt her tenderness and gentleness, otherwise I think my parents' harsh judgemental treatment of me would have made me a sour person. I don't really know what my mom's problem is. Deep down, I think she's just jealous of me and resentful that she didn't have the same opportunities in life."

"Maggie, this takes me back, listening to you talk about all this again. Some things just never change, do they?" He rose and walked to the chair where she was sitting and extended his hand; she took it and he pulled her up and led her back to the couch and then sat down beside her. "But let's talk about less depressing things, shall we?" As he made himself comfortable next to her, his left knee touching her right knee, he put his left arm around her shoulders while he placed his huge right hand on her right knee.

"I am your friend, Maggie," he said, as he began to stroke her knee.

"You know, you're the only person I've ever really been able to share my family story with, Mason."

She laid her head on his shoulder and closed her eyes. She felt safe.

She opened her eyes quickly when she felt his hand fondling her breast. She moved to get up but, before she could rise, Mason had pinned her on the couch. She struggled with him and, as she pushed his muscular body away from her, she fell backwards off the couch and onto the plush carpet. She straightened her dress.

"What are you doing?" she said, her eyes flashing with anger. He had stopped pawing her, she was tidy looking again as she sat on the floor, and he was lying on the couch sideways looking into her eyes. Except for the pushing him away part, this was *deja vu*. Their lovemaking in college had begun just like that. Mason had counted on her responding to him in the same instinctive way as she had long ago.

As she stared back at him, she felt a twinge of resentment. Why had he stirred up this passion between them? As they faced each other, she sitting on the floor, he on the couch, cooling off from the electricity between them, Maggie's thoughts took her back.

More than 20 years ago he had become her first lover. She had been a college sophomore, and he was a junior. Their lovemaking had begun in the tiny room he rented off-campus from a family. Theirs had been a passionate, satisfying relationship. The feelings she felt now seemed the same as long ago. Her reaction to his touch was not changed by time. If she was honest with herself, she felt just as attracted to him now as years ago. But her response to this passion could not be the same now as then.

He finally broke the silence that had been intensified by his piercing stare. His stare was like no other. It was as though his big blue eyes were boring holes through her eye sockets in order to get inside her brain to the exact spot where he might be able to program her feeling and thinking and acting.

"I know you want me, too," he said flatly.

"That's not the point," Maggie replied

softly. "We can't act on every instinct we have or we'd be adulterers, pedophiles, murderers, thieves, you name it. What makes us human is the ability to rise above our instincts, to subdue them if we must. But I'm not telling you anything you don't already know, Mason."

"Maggie, all I want to do is make you feel loved by me just one more time, for old times' sake. What's so wrong with that? No one would know. No one would get hurt."

"We would know. You would know. I would know. Every action we take in life either diminishes us or builds us up. It never leaves us the same. We pay a price for every decision and every action, Mason." She paused, then she continued. "I can't cheat on my children and my husband, Mason," she said. "I really don't even want to cheat on the way I remember our relationship, yours and mine. It was special, and it was powerful, but this is more like lust compared to the pure love we once felt. I don't want to turn the best relationship I ever had into a dirty little secret shared by two middle-aged baby boomers having a mid-life fling."

"The best relationship you ever had?" he echoed. "What about Kurt?"

Maggie wished immediately that she hadn't confessed so much. It would be hard to take back or explain those words. The only escape would be a swift exit.

"Mason, I have to go back to my hotel. It's nearly one A.M. and I'm leaving on a flight at eleven o'clock tonight so I can get back and preach tomorrow."

"You're not cut out to be a minister, Maggie." He was sitting up on the couch now. "You're too honest and outspoken. You won't be able to handle all the compromising that will go into being successful. You're too forthright and truthful."

"Wait a minute, Mason," she smiled. As they were talking, Maggie had gathered her handbag and jacket and walked to the front door with him following her. Now with one hand on the door knob of his apartment entrance she said, "I think I'm flattered, but I also think the qualities you're accusing me of are the ones people expect ministers to have."

She didn't back away when he simply sighed and put his arms around her shoulders and hugged her close to him. It was a sweet, lingering goodbye hug and he held her close for minutes, as though he didn't want to let her go. Maggie could feel his true love.

"If you ever need me, for anything at all, please call me. My Washington and New

York offices will always know where I am." He smiled. "And if you ever need a great criminal attorney, I'm at your service." Then his smile turned to sadness. He was holding her at arm's length now, his hands clutching her shoulders as he looked down into her eyes from his 6' 2" frame. "I love you, baby. I should never have let you go, but if there's a chance we can be together again, I will not let that chance go by. You are my soul mate. I don't know how I let you get away."

She stood on her tiptoes to kiss him on the cheek as she took the business card from his outstretched hand and pushed it into her pocketbook.

"I'm going to be preaching on Amos tomorrow," she smiled. "Take care of yourself and call me if you need help sometime."

"Like sexual therapy-type help?" he asked in mock seriousness.

"No, not like sexual therapy," she smiled. After a final hug at the elevator, she waved goodbye and then the elevator door eclipsed him from view. She wondered on the elevator ride down and then in the taxi when she would see him again.

Everyone was asleep when she got back to the hotel room. She made quick work of brushing her teeth and washing her face and then climbed into bed, exhausted physically and still excited emotionally. No one in years had gotten that close to her raw nerve endings. She hadn't felt that kind of animal passion in so long — both the passion aroused in her for him and the passion she felt from him.

Even though she was a minister, she still had so many philosophical questions. Faith, even strong faith, still leaves questions, and Maggie lay there in her hotel bed with questions about why she wasn't now married to the man she had probably loved the most intensely in her life. It seemed implausible that God would have fated their relationship to take all those twists and turns. It seemed unlikely that God had predestined Mason to simply abandon her one day without warning so that she would rebound into a destructive and abusive relationship. Surely God had not determined that she would divorce, become a single parent, and one day marry again? Perhaps God was just always there, helping to make the best of bad human decisions and always lighting the way back home when the path seemed dark and confusing and scary.

Before she drifted off to sleep, her thoughts raced to the particular classmates she hoped she would see at the Saturday night black-tie affair. She would run into many of her classmates, too, at Saturday's luncheon on the grounds of the B school. She'd have to catch a taxi straight from the party to the airport, but she was booked on the latest flight possible so that she could stay at the dinner socializing for as long as possible. She'd left her car at the airport so if the flight arrived on time at 12:15, she would be home in her own bed by one A.M. She'd be ready to preach the eleven o'clock service on Sunday after a few hours of rest.

AMOS

On the flight, two cups of coffee gave Maggie a second wind. She'd done a lot of work already on the Amos sermon, but she had to polish it on the way home. Her mind was still whirling with impressions of the hundreds of people she'd seen or spoken to at the reunion, but there was no time to analyze or ponder those impressions now. Perhaps she would luck out and have a lazy Sunday afternoon when she could allow her mind to meander back over the past four days. But for now, she would have to work on Amos.

Most Protestant, Roman Catholic, and other denominations including Anglican and Greek Orthodox now shared what they called a "common lectionary," which meant that, every Sunday, ministers all over the world in all denominations were encouraged to read, in common, three different Biblical scriptures selected by an interdenominational team. Of the three readings, one was always an Old Testament reading, one was a reading from one of the four gospels, and the other scripture was usually from the New Testament. The intention of this common lectionary was to focus Christians all over the world on the same issues and themes each Sunday so that some strengthening of Christian solidarity might result.

A preacher did not *have* to use the "common lectionary" but most ministers Maggie knew said the lectionary "kept them honest" and ensured that they did not simply preach their favorite books or their timeworn messages over and over again, to the exclusion of many books of the Bible.

Even if a preacher chose her sermon topic from the common lectionary, she was free to choose among the three scriptures. For that reason, Maggie wondered if most ministers would pick the gospel lesson from Matthew 23:23-36 as their sermon topic rather than the Old Testament reading from Amos 5:21-24. Both were uncharacteristically antagonistic pieces of scripture — the common lectionary invariably seemed to focus more on messages of grace and forgiveness and salvation than on correction and discipline and obedience. There was a third reading from Ephesians 4:17-24 which had a little less of the scorpion's sting in it, so perhaps ministers worldwide tomorrow would be preaching Ephesians.

The sermons that were the most fun to preach were, for Maggie, the ones that let her preach and teach at the same time. And any sermon preached on the book of Amos certainly required some teaching if the preaching was to be understood.

She looked forward to teaching her congregation about this poor shepherd from the barren desert of Tekoa whom God had called twenty-seven centuries ago, and 750 years before the birth of Christ, to prophesy to and pronounce judgement on the very affluent nation called Israel. In 750 B.C. when Amos spoke, Israel consisted of the ten tribes that had revolted in 931 B.C. against the harsh words of King Rehoboam when he attempted to install himself as king of the twelve tribes of Israel after King Solomon's death. In the next 180 years, the ten tribes of Israel had become essentially a separate nation from the other two tribes called Judah, which was all that had been left for King Rehoboam to rule over.

Amos was a great book for dramatic readings because that country boy named Amos from the harsh desert of Tekoa in Judah saw the world and expressed himself in images particular to his desert environment. Lions roaring through the still desert silence as they caught their prey were spoken of matter-of-factly by Amos as he told Israel of God's decision to punish Israel for its neglect of the poor, its corrupt judicial system, its extravagant lifestyle, and its shallow and ritualistic version of religion. No prophet had ever, until Amos, come to the people of Israel to give them the particular message from God that Amos brought, and that message emphasized primarily two things: first, that the God who led them out of slavery in Egypt would not necessarily always protect and defend them militarily, and second, that God did not like all the rituals and ceremonies in their religion because the religion had become "all style, no substance."

So what did this spokesman for God tell Israel that God wanted from them? What God sent Amos to tell Israel was that God wanted the Israelites to treat their fellow men with justice and with righteousness. God wasn't impressed with the fact that the very religious in Israel took their sacrifices frequently to holy shrines like Bethel, where God had spoken to Jacob, and Gilgal, where Joshua had crossed over into the promised land of Canaan after he took over from Moses. Amos was sent to tell a very affluent, very militarily strong, and very religious society that God despised their solemn assemblies and that He wanted them to stop taking advantage of the poor and perverting justice.

The people of Israel in Amos's day were idle and extravagant and filled with great national pride as well as religious zeal. For nearly two hundred years, Israel had grown strong militarily and politically, and they felt that their temples and religious privileges elevated them above other nations. Israel was a very civilized society which believed that God somehow must have been approving of its behavior or else they could not have prospered as they had. The Israelites had a feeling that if you were good, God rewarded you, and they felt they must have been good in God's eyes to have become so well off materially.

But Amos brought a message that God did not respect their civilization and that He regarded their religion as nothing more than empty rituals. There was no purity or honor in their judicial system, Amos told them, and the smallest bribe would motivate a judge to give up a poor man to his wealthy adversary. "You have a false sense of security," Amos told the Israelites, "and God is going to punish you for your lack of principle and inability to do right."

Maggie had always liked the book of Amos, so she looked forward to preaching Amos from the pulpit for the first time. Of all the books in the Bible, though, it was the most "hell-and-brimstone" book and it contained a message that was nearly all correction and judgement. Speaking seven hundred and fifty years before Jesus' birth, Amos had spoken out about so many of the matters that Jesus talked about. In Matthew 23:23 Jesus condemned religious people who "tithe mint and dill and cummin, and have neglected the weightier matters of the law, justice, and mercy, and faith." Jesus was always telling people that, if they wanted to be in a right relationship with God, they first needed to be in right relationships with all of God's creation. Jesus said in Matthew 5:23-24: "So if you are offering your gift at the altar and there remember something that your brother has against you, leave your gift there before the altar and go; first be reconciled to your brother, and then come and offer your gift."

So as the prophet Isaiah foretold the coming of Christ into the world, the prophet Amos looked ahead to the kind of religion Jesus would teach people to practice.

Another prophet, Micah, had warned Israel in this way: "What does the Lord require of you but to do justice, and to love kindness, and to walk humbly with your God."

In expressing God's displeasure with their style of religion, Amos reminded the people of Israel that God had singled them out for special treatment throughout history. As far back as Abraham, God had established a covenant relationship with the Israelites. But what was missing in the religion of Amos's time was any remembrance of the fact that covenant implies God's protection in return for man's obedience.

But the Israelites had forgotten about the "obedience" part of their relationship with God and had come to regard Him as a "sugar daddy" to be fed and flattered. Amos warned them that God did not appreciate their pious rituals and that He insisted that "justice roll down like waters, and righteousness like an everlasting stream."

As always with the messages the prophets brought, the advice was of enormous practical value. And Maggie wanted to convey to her congregation the ultimate sensibility and logic of what Amos said — and Jesus said — about the poor. A society that preys on its poor, that "tramples on the poor," as Amos described it, is just making trouble for itself anyway. We make enemies of those we tyrannize, and the oppression breeds hatred, and hatred always leads people into sin. It is only love that will produce the kind of world we all want to live in, but when the teachings of Jesus and the prophets are brushed aside as unrealistic and idealistic notions, then our world becomes driven by the kind of greed and selfish consumption that characterized the Israeli society Amos was speaking to.

"Think not that I have come to abolish the law and the prophets," Jesus said in Matthew 5:17-20. "I have not come to abolish them but to fulfill them. For truly, I say to you, till heaven and earth pass away, not an iota, not a dot, will pass from the law until all is accomplished. Whosoever then relaxes one of the least of these commandments and teaches men so, shall be called least in the kingdom of heaven; but he who does them and teaches them shall be called great in the kingdom of heaven. For I tell you, unless your righteousness exceeds that of the scribes and Pharisees, you will never enter the kingdom of heaven."

Amos was to hold up a plumb line much as a master builder would do on a piece of construction. Amos said that God had dropped a plumb line on Israel to measure its true religious character, and the plumb line had revealed a poorly constructed society which had to be torn down by the builder.

Suddenly a thought occurred: Maggie suddenly knew how she would present the message of this eighth century B.C. prophet to her twentieth century congregation. She would dramatize the Amos story by writing and then reading "A Letter from Jehovah to the Israelites" which would be a modern translation of the Book of Amos. She would tell her congregation that this is a "pretend" letter which a messenger from God read to the Israelites in the capital city after the king and the chief priest had kicked Amos out of the city because they didn't like what he said.

That's it! That's it! I'll ask the church, Maggie thought, *to pretend they are hearing the letter from Jehovah read to the Israelites by a divine courier after Amos was banished.*

She wrote the letter from Jehovah on the plane trip home. It was a modern translation of Amos from the beginning of chapter one to the end of chapter nine. The words came easily and quickly. Soon the letter was finished with the help of the laptop she'd brought along, so it would take only minutes once she arrived home to get a hard copy to read during the service. She practiced the oral interpretation of the letter by rereading it on the computer screen after she finished writing.

THE SERMON

As she had planned, she began her sermon from the pulpit the next morning by telling her congregation that she would read an imaginary letter from Jehovah brought by a messenger after Amos had been kicked out of Israel.

Dear Israelites:

I bring you a letter from Jehovah. The tone of this letter, and of Jehovah's sentiments, may be summed up in this poem which precedes the letter.

When the Lord roars from Zion,
And when he speaks from Jerusalem,
The pastures of the shepherds mourn,
And the top of Carmel withers.

I shall now begin reading the words Jehovah wishes you to hear. Israel, Jehovah is speaking to you now.

You have heard the words Amos spoke about what's going to happen to the barbarian countries around you. I'm going to bring destruction upon those nations around you that have treated their fellow beings so cruelly. The Syrians, the Philistines, the Phoenicians, the Edomites, the Ammonites, and the Moabites — all those nations around you — their major cities will be consumed by fire and I will not spare even a remnant of those cities.

But Israel and Judah, my greatest wrath is for you. Judah, I'm going to send a fire on the fair city of Jerusalem, the city that has been called "the apple of God's eye." It's a rotten apple now, and I'm going to burn it down since you haven't kept the covenant between us.

And Israel, you've done the same things as Judah and even worse. You people in Israel, you've built a society that I'm ashamed of. You have adopted the philosophy that life is a profit-making venture, and you seem to think that the one that wins in this game of life is the one who has the largest net worth at the end of life. You are so materialistic and greedy that you just trample on the poor and take advantage of them continuously. You've built a society in which you have stacked the decks against the poor in every way. You're in control of every aspect of their lives — how much they pay for food, for rent, for medical treatment, what interest they have to pay when they borrow money — but what you charge them for their necessities in life is inflated and unfair. In every business dealing, the have's take advantage of the have not's. You conduct your business dealings this way, and you couldn't care less how desperate they feel and how frail they are in this high-rent society you have created.

Yet you consider yourself such a cultured and civilized and religious society, don't you, Israel? Yes, you're so religious, aren't you? You've turned holy places like Bethel into places of self-gratification and feasting and socializing. After all I've done for you, Israel! You take what is holy and turn it into something vulgar and tacky, because you're vulgar and tacky, Israel!

I've sent you so many people through the years to try to get you to walk in the right way. I've sent you prophets like Isaiah, and I've sent you great teachers like the Nazarites. But take the Nazarites, for example. What did you do to those Nazarites who were known for their self-discipline and for their well-known vow not to take any alcoholic beverage? What did you do to those Nazarites? Did you learn from them, Israel, as I intended you to? No, you were too busy seducing them! You took those young Nazarites sent to you to be an example of clean living and wholesome conduct and you pressured them into joining your own debauched and selfish lifestyle. So although they were sent to you as examples of the right way to live, you treated their vows and principles as disposable. You are a disposable society, and even the vows you take are disposable. Don't you remember one of the laws I gave to Moses in the wilderness for you? When you make a vow to the Lord your God, you shall not be slack to pay it.

But vows mean nothing to you, Israel. And what did you do to the prophets I sent you? You know that I never do anything in history without revealing it first to my prophets so that they can communicate with you, but what have you done to the prophets I sent you? You've silenced them! You've done to all my prophets what your chief priest Amaziah did to Amos. Amaziah told Amos that he had better go back to Judah, because it wasn't safe for him to come to Bethel anymore to deliver my prophecies.

Well, I'm going to press you down now, Israel. There is a time coming up for you when even your runners will not be able to run and even your brave men will lose their courage.

Oh, how did it come to this? Of all the nations of the earth, Israel, you're the one I have called family. Since I made the covenant with Abraham to make a great nation of him, I have walked with you and have protected you. But I have no other choice now except to bring upon you the great destruction that I have revealed to Amos.

You don't even know how to do the right thing anymore, Israel. So I am going to invite your bitterest enemies — including the hated Egyptians who enslaved you — to come over into the mountains surrounding the great city of yours called Samaria, to see the pathetic crea-

tures you are and the vulgar way you have used the freedom I gave you.

I'm going to punish you, Israel, and I'm going to punish you in front of the nations around you. I'm going to destroy that polluted thing you have turned Bethel into. And you think Jerusalem is near to my heart? What do you think I feel about Bethel? Bethel is the place where I spoke to Jacob, the place where I showed Jacob the ladder reaching up to heaven, and the place where I later renewed with Jacob the covenant I had made with Abraham. And Bethel is the place where I gave Jacob a new name. Bethel is where I told him that he would be called Israel. And look what you've turned Bethel into! It looks like a fun fair! Well, I'm going to bring an end to Bethel; I'm going to bring the altars down; and I'm also going to bring an end to your luxurious living when I tear down your fancy summer houses and winter houses.

You have so many possessions, you rich Israelites. But somewhere along the way you lost sight of the fact that when I give you the power to get great wealth, that means you also have great responsibility. Great wealth should give a person increased opportunities to do good. Sure, there's a pleasure in accumulating things, but there's a greater pleasure in giving.

But that's not the path you have followed, Israel.

And the ones in your society who have disappointed me in the bitterest way are the women. You know, the women in a society are usually the people who can be counted on to hear the cries of the poor and needy. Women are often the most tenderhearted in society. They're the heart and conscience of society. Women are the ones who go through childbirth and who are the most tuned in to the weakest members of society. They have a special knack for expressing something very close to divine love. But . . . not the women in Israel! The women in Israel are just a bunch of greedy, materialistic animals who can't get enough of anything — money, drink, food, houses, you name it. They have pushed their husbands to make more money, be commercially successful, and they don't care how their husbands make the money. If they end up adding to their property because a poor man lost his job and then his house, the women don't care. It's fair game to take advantage of someone's misfortune.

You know, Israel, there aren't many creatures in the animal kingdom that I created that oppress their fellow creatures the way you oppress your fellow creatures. You have made a business out of preying on your fellow man. Lions have spared men, as in the case of Daniel in the lion's den. Ravens have fed men, as they fed Elijah in the wilderness. Yet, you Israelites have created a society where one man seeks to eat up and devour another. Dogs don't eat dogs, but you humans try to prey on and eat up and devour one another.

Oh, but you just love to come to Bethel to bring me your offerings and your sacrifices. You foolish people! Do you think you can fool me? Do you think I am impressed by the generous offerings you bring me when I know that you have robbed and cheated people to get those offerings? How dare you come to Bethel with your holy, pious expressions to bring me what you have looted from the poor? And do you think I have anything but contempt for the employer who oppresses his workers six days of the week and then goes to church twice on the Sabbath?

And please, Israel, don't try to claim that you don't know what I mean when I talk about oppression of the poor. Oppression of the poor is any cowardly and shameful advantage that a man takes of human weakness. It's cheating someone in business. It's having sex with an innocent child. It's profiting because of someone else's misfortune. And it's watching the smallest and weakest members of society get oppressed without doing anything about it. It's letting it happen while you graze like cows on the fatness of life.

Feebleness, poverty, childhood, old age — those are supposed to move you to pity, but in-

stead you oppress the feeble and the poor for your own gain or pleasure, and that is an outrage against a primary law that I have planted in your conscience.

And you stupid people! You assume that the poor man and the helpless child whom you take advantage of have no friends in high places, Israel. How wrong you are! Don't you know that all the oppressed have a friend and an avenger in God?

Don't you understand that your oppression of the poor, your taking advantage of the weak, is an offense against God's laws? I have distinctly commanded you to LOVE your neighbor as yourself. When you oppress the poor and overlook the needy, you kindle my deepest disgust and indignation.

And I'd be curious to know what you Israelites imagine you would say to your God about your oppression of others on that Day of the Lord that you think you're looking forward to? What would you say, Israel? "Oh, Lord, we thought you were too great to notice what men did on earth." *Or,* "Lord, we took advantage of them because they were weak, and we saw that we could make a good profit out of their defenselessness."

Well, Israel, I am not a distant king. I am a Father who is prompt to feel and to avenge the wrongs of my children. How would you Israelites feel if one of your children tramples on another? How do you feel when your neighbor's children crush your children? You can judge from your own feelings how your God feels when He sees men preying on their fellow men.

Oh, Israel, I've sent you so many signs along the way to try to wake you up. Remember how I sent floods on one city and a drought on another city? But you paid no attention. Besides, you had plenty of money so that you could recover quickly from a disaster. No big deal. And then I sent diseases to humble you. I had your gardens and crops destroyed by mildew and pests. But nothing I did woke you up and humbled you and made you return to me.

So this is what I'm going to do, Israel. You'd better listen closely, Israel: prepare to meet your God. Prepare to meet the One who created everything!

I am going to break out like a fire and I am going to rage throughout Israel. I am going to devour your people who have turned justice into rotting wood. I am going to punish you and publicly humiliate you because of the way you have discarded anything to do with living in a right relationship with the One who created you from dust.

You just hate people who tell the truth, don't you, Israel? You just had to drive Amos out of Israel, didn't you, because he told you the truth and he told you what you needed to hear. You despise anyone who offers you any kind of correction.

I have seen every sin and every evil deed you have done, Israel. And I am telling you, you're not going to live in those fine houses that your dishonesty and oppression have built.

You claim that you are really looking forward to the Day of the Lord, don't you, Israel? Are you serious? Are you for real? That's not going to be a happy day for you! That's not going to be a day when Israel and Judah get reunited and the twelve tribes will again have a great king like David or Solomon. The Day of the Lord that's coming your way is going to be a day of darkness and gloom!

And let me tell you this, Israel. You know what really makes me sick? I can't stand those holy days, those religious holidays of yours, when you try to act so solemn and pious and when you bring me the things that you have looted and cheated and robbed people to get. I hate your feasts and your solemn assemblies!

What I want is what the prophets have been telling you. I want justice to roll down like water rolling down a mountain, and I want the unpolluted waters of righteousness to flood like a stream throughout all of society.

All of you people who feel so at ease in Zion, who feel so complacent, all you people who lie so comfortably on your silk sheets and ivory furniture and eat only the finest delicacies, all you who play only idle music to satisfy your sensual pleasures, listen up. You who consider yourselves at the head of society will be the first to go into the brutal exile and captivity that I am going to allow.

It's a sad day that's coming to you, Israel. When ten people living together in one house die, the distant relative who has to come to bury them will be afraid to mention my name lest he rekindle God's anger upon himself!

I'm going to raise up a nation against you militarily, Israel, and you will know what oppression feels like. "The measure you give will be the measure you get," *Israel, as it is written in the scriptures.*

You remember what Amos told you about the visions I sent him? I sent him a vision saying that I would send an army of locusts to devour the land. But Amos pleaded with me and I reconsidered. And then I sent Amos a vision showing a fire scorching the land. But Amos pleaded with me and again I reconsidered. But when I, the master builder of everything, held up a plumb line to this dishonest and corrupt society, I saw I had no choice but to tear it down. Then I showed Amos how Israel is just like a basket of rotten fruit. And what can you do with rotten fruit except throw it out?

Don't you know, Israel, that I see through your hypocrisy? Don't you know that I can see how you just can't wait for the Sabbath to end so that you can start making money again using your crooked weights, inflated prices, inferior goods, and misleading information?

And I am angered by something else that showed up when I held up the plumb line, Israel. I saw the lack of justice in your society. You know, in any society the rulers and the judges are more or less in the place of God. Human law should exist so that order can be preserved and public morality guarded. Those who administer the law in any society are really standing in for God, who is the fountain of all law and morality.

But what I saw, Israel, when I held up the plumb line, is that your judges and your rulers have abused their positions and they have dishonored the divine concept of justice. What your society has done, Israel, is to prostitute the lofty principle of justice and divine government. Justice is like a street walker that is for sale.

And when the judicial system is corrupt, when men get the justice they can afford, *when justice is for sale, then the innocent are without defense and there is no restraint of wickedness.*

I will not forget what you have done, Israel, and I will make the Day of the Lord like a day of mourning for an only son. I will turn your feasts and your solemn assemblies into funerals, and I will transform your singing into sadness.

I will send a famine on your land. But this time it won't be a famine of food or water. The famine I'm going to send will be a famine of hearing the words of the Lord. I'm not going to send prophets, I'm not going to send teachers, I'm not going to dial your number, and I'm not going to answer the phone when you call. Your young men and your young women, your sons and your daughters, your grandchildren and your great grandchildren, will thirst for a relationship with me again, but it will be a thirst that will not be quenched. They will yearn to hear the kind of words that could help them get back into a right relationship with their God, but I will be silent, and I will not speak.

One day I will restore the fortunes of Israel and raise up the remnant in order to keep the promise I made to Abraham. One day I will permit Israel to rebuild the ruined cities and replant their gardens. But before that restoration, there will be a judgement.

THE RESPONSE

The furor that followed the Amos sermon was unexpected. Objectively, Maggie knew when she wrote it that it was an indictment of society. But, after all, the sermon was simply a modern translation and dramatization of a short book written by "the Prophet of Doom" more than twenty-seven centuries ago.

But objectively was not the way church members reacted to the Amos sermon. Even on their way out of church that morning, many members exhibited unusual coldness or left through the side entrance of the church instead of shaking hands with her on the way out of the narthex, as was their custom. There were a few enthusiastic "thank you's" but there had been very few. Mostly there seemed an attitude of stunned disbelief or hostility among members as they left the sanctuary.

By Monday afternoon Maggie had been called not only by the district superintendent but also by the bishop of the conference. And when the bishop calls, something's up.

The bishop didn't take very long to say what he had to say. There had been an outpouring of complaints about the appropriateness of her Amos sermon, and he wanted her to go on voluntary administrative leave until the matter could be investigated. He asked for a copy of the controversial letter she had read. While on administrative leave, she would continue to be paid her normal salary and receive her regular benefits, but the parishioners were in an uproar and felt hostile toward her now because of that sermon, the bishop told her.

Bill Farmer, the church's "real" minister, was on a flight home from Saudi Arabia at that very moment, the bishop also told her, and he would be resuming charge of his church by midweek. The conflict in the Middle East was over except for the long process of withdrawing troops, and Reverend Farmer was needed more to handle the current crisis at Golgotha than to assist the victims of war.

The bishop made no apologies, no predictions, and no editorial comments. When she hung up, Maggie realized she had never felt so much in limbo. She felt disconnected from every life support system that normally sustained her.

She hadn't been fired, she kept telling herself. Not exactly. But she had essentially been told to "clear out her desk" and vacate her office immediately until further notice.

What had happened? Why did the church members react so violently to Amos's message? What exactly had provoked the church members so much that they had apparently conspired to have Maggie removed from her job?

An hour later, Maggie had her belongings and papers in a large box she had asked Martha to fetch her. Obviously the bishop had briefed Martha even before he had spoken to Maggie, because Martha clearly saw that Maggie was packing up, and yet she asked no questions. Martha did look sad and in pain, however, and it was a welcome sign to see that someone seemed distressed that she was leaving.

It was Maggie's philosophy in life to always try to make the best of everything, and she thought as she was driving home about how she would make the best of this bitter hurt and rejection.

For some reason she didn't understand, Maggie found herself quite frequently at the center of a storm that she had inadvertently stirred up. So it wasn't a new feeling to discover that there was a heated controversy swirling around her because of something she'd done or said quite innocently. She never said or did anything to intentionally provoke controversy, but for some reason controversy was the product of her words and actions from time to time. She sometimes felt that God must have a hard job for her to do at some point in the future, and that He was toughening her up for it by these minor skirmishes in life.

A sense of relief came over her as she walked into her front door and realized that she was home, for good, for the day. What a feeling of freedom to know that she didn't have a church meeting to attend tonight. She felt excited that she would be able to meet her children at their bus stop after school and work with them on homework without a deadline hanging over her head. To have the luxury of being a mommy all day long for a while was a delicious thought.

Ashley was jubilant when she saw her mother at the bus stop, and she took her hand as they were walking home as though she never intended to let it go. She was sitting at the kitchen table helping Ashley with second grade homework when Jonathan arrived home. He seemed just as thrilled to see her as Ashley had been, and he became a nonstop chatterbox as soon as he hit the door. Within ten minutes of his arriving home, Maggie knew who had been throwing condoms filled with water on the school bus, how the fund-raiser candy had been stolen from a dozen lockers, why the elephant crossed the road, and exactly how the fourth grade teachers were planning to bend the rules to sneak in the classroom holiday parties which were not allowed by school policy.

The first few minutes after the kids arrived home from school were precious and unique, because they always spilled their guts and told her everything about their day. After that, they forgot it and by the time evening rolled around, a few hours of homework had erased the day from their memory.

It did strike Maggie as more than coincidental — was it fate? — that her housekeeper had just left town for a month of vacation to visit her son in Arizona. At the time they had discussed the vacation, Maggie and Kurt had figured they would be struggling through her vacation and juggling their schedules to meet Jonathan and Ashley's bus and stay with them until thirteen-year-old Brent got home from school. In the eighth grade, Brent was old enough to supervise his two siblings for an hour or so if necessary, but then the children had so many activities after school that they needed the taxi service Mrs. Darcey also was paid to provide.

Kurt had expected Maggie to meet the kids after school that day, so he was completely taken by surprise by the news she gave him once the kids were in bed. After she read the two littlest ones a story and tucked them in, she gave Brent a kiss on the forehead and told him to turn his lights out soon. He had an algebra test the next day and would be studying another half hour or so.

Downstairs in the family room adjoining their bedroom, Kurt was reading the paper with the television on in the background. He looked up and smiled at her as she came into the room. She smiled back.

"How was the reunion?" he asked.

They had barely had a moment together to really talk since she'd arrived back from Boston in the early dawn Sunday. Then she had preached the Amos sermon, which he had complimented her on, and they had spent a quiet Sunday afternoon reading the paper, playing with the children, and napping. It was only Monday and the reunion already seemed months ago.

"Great. Everyone missed you and sent their regards."

She walked over to the couch where he was sitting and sat down beside him. He looked up. He had expected her to get lost in the household chores — making the children's lunches, tidying the kitchen, laying out the cereal and dishes for tomorrow's breakfast, folding laundry — as she usually did at night. There was nothing very glamorous about the lifestyle of a professional woman. Usually Maggie would work all day and come home to work all night. Mrs. Darcey was a good after-school nanny to the kids but she was hopeless on the cleaning and other chores so Maggie had to do them after the kids went to bed.

"Did you have trouble getting off to meet the kids today?" he asked.

Maggie smiled. "No, it was easy. I think I was fired today. At least that's what it felt like. What they said was that I am on administrative leave for a few weeks or until further notice."

"What?"

Obviously he was shocked. She started at the beginning and told him every word the bishop had said. Apparently there had been considerable resentment and negativism produced by her hard-hitting sermon on Sunday, and the bishop relieved her of responsibilities at Golgotha and summoned the senior minister to return home since the war had been declared officially over.

"But what's going to happen, Maggie? I've got some houses for sale and some things are beginning to pop for me professionally here.

I thought we were coming here so that you could eventually become an understudy to this senior minister for a few years once the war settled down. I don't know if we can financially handle the burden of moving right now if the bishop decides to move you to a new church because of the politics here."

Maggie felt her stomach knotting up inside her as she focused on the particular kind of pain that financial pressure is. "I know you don't want to move now, Kurt. I don't want to move either. But I haven't done anything wrong. All I did was preach a sermon to communicate the thoughts of an Old Testament prophet who lived twenty-seven centuries ago!"

"Apparently they didn't want to hear that sermon, Maggie," he replied flatly.

"Maybe they *didn't* want to hear that sermon. *Obviously* they didn't want to hear that sermon! But I absolutely refused then, and I refuse now, to compromise or dilute any message in the scriptures. You know, Kurt, I can feel my Irish temper flaring up all of a sudden. I don't feel sorry for myself that people are upset with me. I just feel damned irritated that some people want to oppress the message of correction that the church has to speak on occasion if it's honest. I mean, this religion isn't only about grace and love. Jesus Christ didn't specialize in cheap grace. His grace is costly, and I won't cheapen what he did when he visited this planet by speaking some watered-down version of the Good Book."

He smiled and pulled her toward him on the couch so that her right leg was touching his left leg while his left arm circled her shoulders. He leaned his head against hers and laid his right hand on top of hers.

"That's my girl," he said softly. "That's what I've always loved about you, Maggie," he said, squeezing her shoulder gently. "You never cheapen the product you're selling. You're the real thing, honey, and I love you for it. I don't want you to do anything except what you think is right. We'll figure out how to make the finances work."

"Oh, Kurt," Maggie groaned, laying her head back on the couch and snuggling nearer to him, "you and the kids are my sanctuary in this tough old world."

She leaned against his shoulder for nearly twenty minutes as they became absorbed in a rerun of a "Cheers" program on the television which had been on in the background. Then she excused herself to go into the bathroom adjoining their bedroom to take a leisurely bath. It was truly a pleasure not having any book work or preparation or, worse yet, a church meeting that evening. As she lay in the bath luxuriating in bubbles and hot water, she looked up to see him staring down at her.

"Did you check the kids? Are they asleep?" she asked.

"Sure are," he smiled. "Maggie, you are beautiful. And I do want you tonight, baby. I'm going to take a shower."

Maggie was in their bed waiting for him when he returned from the shower smelling like Brut and baby powder. He turned off the light before climbing into bed. Maggie went to sleep that night with a sense of security at her core that she hadn't felt in a long time. Married sex could be very satisfying and reaffirming. There was a tranquility about lying next to the same person every night.

For the next seven days Maggie was left alone by the outside world, and it was glorious being able to just be a mom without being distracted by a million cares and worries. Kurt came home for lunch every day, and they had a chance to talk and laugh in a way that they hadn't in a long time. In spite of the fact that there was a cloud hanging over her head, Maggie felt as though she were on holiday. But it did seem like a strange coincidence that this career misfortune had befallen her just when Mrs. Darcey was on an extended vacation.

It was nearly lunchtime one day during the second week of her "semi-retirement" when the phone rang. The caller introduced himself as Dr. Bill Farmer. He was brief, and his tone was reserved.

"Mrs. Dillitz?"

"Yes, this is Mrs. Dillitz. Who is calling, please?"

"This is Dr. William Farmer, Mrs. Dillitz. I've returned from the Middle East and am back in the driver's seat at Golgotha. I had a long discussion with the bishop by phone today about what we should do with you, and I thought we should arrange a time to sit down and talk together."

They agreed to meet the next day for lunch at a small Italian restaurant in town. He suggested the time and location because, as he told her, it seemed advisable to him that they "get together away from the scene of the crime." He laughed when he said it, but Maggie felt embarrassed, guilty, threatened, insecure, and invaded by what seemed like a taunting and humiliating remark.

Wednesday was a wet windy day, and Maggie felt chilled to the bone waiting outside the Olive Garden. Suddenly she saw a tall, husky man with broad shoulders walking toward the restaurant. She checked her watch. It was the right time but the wrong man. The man coming toward her must be a football coach or something like that. As his broad shoulders came close to her, the man's face erupted into a smile. He was a handsome, fiftyish fellow with only a hint of grey hair concentrated near the cowlick in his closely cut hair.

"Maggie?"

"Yes," she replied, returning the smile of the man whose identity she could not figure out.

"I'm Dr. Farmer, Maggie. Let's go inside." He put his arm around her waist and guided her into the warmth of the restaurant reeking with the smells of olive oil, garlic, and rich sauces.

He was gracious and warm to her as they ordered. He frequently reached over to pat her outstretched hand as it lay on the table, as if to comfort and reassure her. They exchanged pleasantries and made small talk during lunch, but when the coffee arrived, he got down to business.

"Well, Maggie," he began, "the bishop isn't sure what we should do with you. You've alienated a lot of the congregation at Golgotha by that sermon on Amos. You know, our congregation isn't real accustomed to women teaching, much less preaching. I guess I'm from the 'Old School,' Maggie, but I don't think women are supposed to try to do what men are called to do in the church."

Maggie studied his tanned face and chiseled good looks. He was very handsome and rugged looking, like a cowboy. But behind that pretty face was a man with an unattractive vision of how women fit into the social order. Maggie decided to probe into his philosophy.

"What do you mean, Dr. Farmer? What aren't women supposed to do?"

"Well, young lady, I think you know that in Paul's first letter to Timothy, he says it very clearly: 'I permit no woman to teach or have authority over men; she is to keep silent.' "

"Well, Dr. Farmer, don't you think times have changed a little since Paul was writing? He was an eccentric old bachelor anyway, and he said a lot of things that we don't exactly have to hold up as a steadfast article of faith. I mean, he said in I Corinthians that 'it's degrading for a man to have long hair.' And he also said, 'it's better not to marry.' And he encouraged us in I Timothy to 'use a little wine for the sake of your stomach.' Now, I'm not sure that we need to all take up drinking just to make sure we're honoring the words of that old Apostle."

Dr. Farmer smiled, then probed, "Tell me more about what you think, Maggie. I'd be interested in hearing what they teach at Yale Divinity School."

"I think we must be prepared to honor the fact that God is clearly calling women into ministry, just as we need to honor most of what was said by that wonderful old missionary. I think the second of the great Ten Commandments speaks to this point when it says we shall not make any graven images and shall not bow down to them or serve them. We cannot literally make every word of Paul into a graven image that we bow down to, especially if honoring those words forces us into the position of being the 'judge and jury' of our fellow men."

Dr. Farmer was listening without any particular emotion expressed on his face. She continued.

"It is not for us to judge who God calls. God calls whomever he wishes, and it is not for us to question the sex or credentials of those He calls. We have to be careful about the judgements we make about people because of their sex or their background. That's just what people did in Amos's day, too. They questioned the fact that a poor, dumb shepherd was being sent to bring a message to the prosperous nation of Israel. The scriptures make it very clear that He 'chooses what is weak in the world to confound the wise.' Even if someone thought women were lowly in the social order, God Himself will call women into leadership in His kingdom as He wishes. If you want to know what I think about Paul, I honor that old Apostle, but I don't agree with the way his words are interpreted today to discriminate against women called to pulpit ministries. What Paul said about women may have been a practical working philosophy in his day, and it may even have been something he was trying to say to a particular group of women in Corinth who were making trouble, but he spoke those words twenty centuries ago, and it does seem clear that God is calling women into ministry in very great numbers. Nearly half of all divinity school students today are women, Dr. Farmer."

The waitress arrived and Dr. Farmer ordered more coffee for both of them as he laid his credit card on the table next to the check.

"Now, Maggie," he said, changing the subject abruptly, "I have to discuss a more serious subject with you."

"Oh? More serious than that, Dr.

Farmer?" she replied in mock seriousness. "What is that, sir?" Apparently he felt her point of view was too contrary to even merit a response. She wondered if he'd actually listened to anything she said.

"The bishop is looking to me for counsel on what to do with you. Your career is more or less in my hands at the moment, you might say. And I'm not sure what I should say to the bishop. Should you be transferred back to an administrative post? Should I keep you here under my wing? What is the proper remedy for the difficult situation you've placed us in now?"

"Dr. Farmer," she began with a respectful tone in her voice, "why is there so much controversy over a silly little sermon?"

He smiled as he began. "My dear Maggie, there is probably much sentiment that, as a woman, you should really not be in the pulpit preaching at all, that you simply don't belong there. Then you add to that sentiment the fact that you preached a message of harsh judgement and correction to a lot of pretty good folks who are now up in arms. You really managed to stir up a hornet's nest among the Junior Leaguers at our church. They're a group of pretty powerful women, and they're downright, flat-out angry that you have accused them of being so callous.

They thoroughly resented being called 'fat cows,' Maggie, although I must say I find that very amusing personally." He had a big grin on his face.

" 'Fat cows of Bashan' is precisely what Amos called the Israeli women he was talking to. I never really said it that way in my sermon."

"Well, anyway, Maggie, you have offended many of the movers and shakers in the church. What do *you* think we should do with you?"

"I do not wish to be transferred at this time, Dr. Farmer. My husband is rather pregnant with several houses he's building and it would be a terrible time to move him or the children. I'm not afraid to stay here and face the controversy, Dr. Farmer. I haven't done anything wrong, and I don't feel ashamed."

"So you would have me advise the bishop to leave you here, under my watchful eye?"

"If that's the way you want to put it, Dr. Farmer, I suppose so. I don't want to move again now. It's terribly inconvenient. I mean, it could just lead to our financial ruin, not to mention marital problems."

As they left the restaurant Dr. Farmer told Maggie he would be speaking with the bishop in the next week and would call her soon.

The next week of being a mom at home was a fulfilling one for Maggie. Being at home when the kids got home from school was the best part. It was a luxury to be able to be a wife and mother unfettered by the constantly changing priorities of pastoring and counseling and managing people. She was aware it would not last long, so she was determined to savor the freedom completely while it lasted.

Exactly a week later Dr. Farmer called. It was about a quarter of nine in the morning and Maggie had just returned from driving the two younger children to school.

"Maggie?" said the familiar voice, "Bill Farmer here. I've gone to bat for you with the bishop." He paused.

"I appreciate that, Dr. Farmer," she said warmly.

"Here's what I've worked out with him, Maggie. You will come back to work here at Golgotha as our Director of Education. I think I can smooth things out, and I think most people will accept you in that role. You'll be working with the Sunday School program, some youth programs, and most of our special projects like Bible School and summer camps. How does that sound?"

"Oh, well, that sounds fine, I guess. I mean, I certainly appreciate your wanting to have me on your staff."

"There's more, Maggie," he continued. "The bishop is concerned about the hurricane that has just devastated Jamaica. He wants to send me to lead a work team for two weeks, and I have suggested that he make you a part of that work team. You can't really stay here in a leadership role at the church while I'm gone. That won't work just now. But you might as well be involved in productive work since you're on the payroll anyway. Have you ever been on a mission work team, Maggie?"

"No, I haven't," Maggie said slowly, thinking of the logistics involved in leaving the children. At least Mrs. Darcey would be back at the end of next week, so it could theoretically work. The parsonage which the church provided for them was a huge old house with six bedrooms, so Mrs. Darcey always had a bedroom on the occasions when she did sleep over to supervise the children. Since she was a widow, she had the flexibility to move into their home for short periods of time when Maggie and Kurt were out of town.

"Maggie? Are you there?" Dr. Farmer was waiting for her response.

"Yes, I'm sorry, sir. I was just thinking. You've said so much, and my mind is racing ahead to some of the details of implementing all this."

"Then you are in basic agreement?"

"Yes, I am. I think what you're proposing makes good use of me as a resource. I guess I have temporarily lost my ability to pastor at Golgotha. Being on a work team could be fun and rewarding. I've been to Jamaica twice with my husband. His father was in diplomatic service when he was young, so he went to elementary and junior high school in Jamaica at a private school called The Priory School. I love Jamaica, and I'd love to help the Jamaicans recover from Hilda."

"Well, that's great, Maggie. No planes can get in and out of the airports on the island right now, so you'll have a few days to get ready. But pack your bags, and we'll meet at the airport next Thursday. We'll be gone about two weeks. I'll have my secretary make the reservations and she'll call you later to confirm the itinerary."

On the flight to Jamaica, Maggie's thoughts were of Kurt and the children. Kurt had been very sweet. He had encouraged her to make the trip. He thought it would be an amicable, compliant gesture toward the professional clergy who were in charge of her future, and he told Maggie she would love being back in Paradise, Kurt's pet name for Jamaica. Having spent much of his youth growing up in Jamaica, Kurt had always told her that it had, indeed, been like growing up in Paradise. And he and Maggie had never had happier times than their times in Jamaica. Jamaica was where they had enjoyed the most intimate sexual experiences, shared the deepest personal feelings, and laughed the heartiest laughs during the years they'd known each other. The first time they had gone to Jamaica was on their honeymoon; then they had managed to take several family vacations on the island during the nearly eleven years they'd been married. Going to Jamaica without Kurt felt like going on a honeymoon without a lover. Nevertheless, Jamaica would still be Jamaica, and Maggie felt her excitement mounting to see the familiar silhouette of that large Caribbean island with its gracious mountain ranges rising above white sandy beach playgrounds.

But Jamaica was not all playground along the coast. Jamaica certainly had its world-famous oases where the sun always shone and where the weary from Japan, France, England, America, Germany, and other lands could bask in tropical summer weather year round. But Kurt had introduced Maggie to places off the beaten track and away from the "name-brand" tourist havens like Montego Bay, Negril, and Ocho Rios. The first thing Kurt always did after he got off the plane and cleared immigration was rent a car, and then he and Maggie would be off exploring the island, poking around the bays Christopher Columbus had sailed into five hundred years ago, and eating with the native Jamaicans at the pork pits that are the open-air, spicy chicken-pork equivalents of America's hamburger joints.

Someone's hand began affectionately rubbing the top of her hand as Maggie stared out the airplane window at the white cumulus clouds floating by in the sea-blue sky. Maggie turned to see Dr. Farmer searching her face. She gently pulled her hand away.

"You have been so lost in thought, dear,"

he chided her. "Did you forget you have a companion?"

Maggie smiled weakly at him but before she could respond, the Air Jamaica stewardess was beside their row handing them immigration documents and landing cards to fill out. They both got busy filling out the paperwork required to cross international borders.

Maggie caught a glimpse of Montego Bay just before they landed, and it looked as though the land below was strewn with the carnage of ravaged vegetation. The pilot warned them that there was emergency power providing electricity on the island, but Jamaica had been completely without power for two weeks after the hurricane. It was only yesterday, the pilot told them, that the U.S. Corps of Engineers had succeeded in rigging up some emergency power in the major cities of Montego Bay and Kingston, but the alternate power supply was unreliable and erratic. Departing passengers had better prepare themselves for very little hot water and few of the other luxuries they were accustomed to. Theirs was an early morning flight which would get them into "Mobay" at mid-afternoon.

A contingent of Peace Corps workers was also on the plane and, after they landed, Dr.

Farmer and the head of the Peace Corps groups struck up a conversation as they all lined up to clear immigration. It seemed they all had reservations for the same hotel — the Doctor's Cave in downtown Mobay — so they would all travel together by an airport bus to the hotel. On the crowded ride to Doctor's Cave, Maggie could see the ravages of Mother Nature. The main streets were still littered with tree limbs, and everywhere she looked, nearly everything looked rearranged in a most untidy way.

It was nearly dusk by the time they were checking into the hotel, and the Doctor's Cave had candles in every nook and cranny. Maggie was glad the Peace Corps group was staying there, too. They were a happy, fun-loving group of former school teachers, psychologists, and other professionals who ranged in age from twenty-five to sixty-five. They were told at check-in that, because of the power shortage and very probable blackout that night, the Doctor's Cave was offering a buffet for only two hours, from seven to nine. They all agreed to meet downstairs at seven o'clock.

The buffet was scrumptious, although it was more like a cold salad bar than a dinner meal. Kippers, tuna, and other canned items were the menu items, in addition to fresh fruit. Refrigeration had been a rarity in Jamaica for two weeks, so ice was nearly unavailable. Everything was at room temperature, including the water, beer, and rum punch. The Peace Corps group, like Maggie and Dr. Farmer, was scheduled for a mandatory two-day briefing at the American Embassy in Kingston in forty-eight hours, so they would all have to make a long, slow bus ride from Montego Bay to Kingston the next day.

On the way to Kingston, Maggie observed a debris-strewn coastline and ravaged coconut orchards. The hurricane had not caused a lot of deaths, and it had not picked only one city on the island to torment, but what it had done was probably much worse. It had simply trashed the whole island. The clean up would probably take two years, most people on the bus were estimating — that is, if international relief organizations provided the money and manpower for the clean up. That's what Dr. Farmer, Maggie, and the Peace Corps troupe were doing there. They were part of the first "A Team" sent in to aid in the clean up. Maggie and Dr. Farmer would only be offering "moral support" for the two weeks they would be there, but the Peace Corps people would be there for at least a year and, after the Embassy briefing, they would be assigned to various towns and cities throughout the island.

The drive from Montego Bay to Kingston, the country's capital, took a whole day, about three times as long as normal because of the frequent bobbing and weaving by the bus to avoid tree parts that had been violently thrown into the road by Mother Nature. By dusk, they were pulling into the Courtleigh Manor, an elegant old Jamaican hotel in the heart of the downtown. Again they were informed at check-in that the dinner meal would be served buffet-style between six-thirty and eight-thirty because of the unreliable nature of the emergency power supply. Of course, Jamaican time was a well known joke, and if a Jamaican ever told you that he would "soon come," you could only assume that it would probably happen on that same day. Dinner times in the aftermath of a hurricane would no doubt be even more uncertain.

An unexpected source of pleasure on the trip for Maggie was the presence of the lively Peace Corps group. They were continuously cracking jokes and livening up what could have seemed an important but somber duty.

The next morning everyone seemed to have the same idea: have a breakfast of tropical fruit while basking in the warm sun beside one of the Courtleigh Manor's two pools. Inside the Courtleigh Manor, one could almost forget about the devastation throughout the countryside. Here in the country's capital, the tourist trade at least seemed like "business as usual." They got word at lunchtime that their briefing at the embassy would be delayed another day, so the Peace Corps crowd began making plans to do some sightseeing in the afternoon. The hotel's minibus took a group of eighteen, including Maggie, to see Port Royal.

Once a den of thieves and pirates, Port Royal had been called "the wickedest city in the world." On its site an earthquake had occurred four hundred years ago that legend said was an act of God to punish the sinful city. At Port Royal Maggie and the others saw tomb stones erected by the families of young naval officers who had died of Yellow Fever, and one tomb stone immortalized a man who, the stone said, had survived the fever and was actually swallowed up and then spat out again by the earthquake.

Standing near the tip of the bay jutting out into the Caribbean, Maggie could sense the history of this beautiful island. The Spanish and English had fought over the island, but neither the Spanish nor English had been willing to risk much to capture Jamaica. Indeed, the pirates were able to thrive on the open seas in the sixteenth and seventeenth centuries because the pirates did "the dirty work" that the Spanish and English navies did not want to do.

Christopher Columbus had happened upon Jamaica around 1494 and claimed it for Spain. Queen Isabella had given Jamaica to Columbus as a gift and the island remained in Columbus's family until 1527 or so, although none of Columbus's descendants ever visited the island. Over the next couple of hundred years, hardly any of the nobility from England or Spain wanted to risk a precarious ocean voyage to visit a country populated by a few Arawak Indians and totally lacking in the luxuries and pageantry of the royal courts back in London and Madrid. In those days, an ocean voyage was a life-threatening adventure anyway, so the ownership of an island like Jamaica was of dubious value. If one could never go there without putting one's life at risk to typhoid or Yellow Fever, what was the point?

Still, the Caribbean islands had offered the lure of gold to hardy travelers so the most adventuresome took to the seas to try to hunt for gold in Hispaniola, Jamaica, and the other islands discovered and named by Columbus.

Those adventurers found no gold in Jamaica but they did find an island that could be farmed for certain things. Columbus had brought sugar cane to the island, and banana and pineapple were growing there already. The Spanish after 1525 tried to turn the Arawaks into slaves, because farming the sugar cane, banana, and pineapple was a most labor-intensive operation. The Arawaks did not thrive on slavery, however. Those laid-back Indians who had invented the hammock rapidly died under the rigors of forced labor combined with the diseases the Spanish introduced to the island.

The English took Jamaica from the Spanish in 1655 as almost an afterthought. The English had been rebuffed in their attempt to take Hispaniola from the Spanish, so the British invaded the island of Jamaica and chased the Spanish governor out through the Runaway Bay underground tunnels. The Spanish had fled to Cuba and to Hispaniola and to other islands.

The English continued to farm Jamaica for its pineapples, bananas, sugar cane, coffee, and pimento, but the farming of the island demanded yet more labor. So the English continued the slave trade established by the Spanish. English ships would leave London loaded with basic foodstuffs and necessities; the ships would land in Africa where the foodstuffs would be exchanged for human beings; then the blacks would be taken from their homeland on a perilous ocean voyage to Jamaica, where they would be sold as slaves in exchange for the bananas, pineapple, sugar cane, coffee, and spices so heavily in demand in England. When the merchant ships unloaded their expensive produce in London or Bristol, they would load up again with basic foodstuffs and begin the three-part journey again.

So Jamaica became an English-speaking country of black slaves, while pirates ruled the seas because the English and Spanish navies felt sea duty was too hazardous. The English used the pirates to their advantage. The pirate Henry Morgan was made Governor General of Jamaica in an attempt to claim for the crown what Henry Morgan had taken from Spain by legitimizing his successful plundering. And Henry Morgan's home had been at Port Royal.

In the nineteenth century the British Parliament finally ended slavery after extensive public outcries by missionaries and other humanists. The Jamaicans then toiled in much the same way for many years. The banana and pineapple plantations stayed in the hands of a few rich English families, and some smart Syrian, Lebanese, and Chinese immigrants developed the island's retail businesses. Maggie knew that now the island produced bananas, pineapples, coffee, and tropical spices for export and farming was capital-intensive.

Most modern Jamaicans were involved in the tourist industry in some way, so that was what Maggie and the others were doing there. Unless Jamaica could quickly recover from the hurricane and restore its tourist industry, there would be mass unemployment that would produce a nation of beggars.

Yes, power had to be restored to Jamaica. But it was work and jobs and employment and tourism and "business as usual" that had to be restored to Jamaica as soon as possible.

Kurt had told her about how Jamaica was simply a rock if you could look underneath it — quite literally, a rock sitting in the middle of the Caribbean. Just stepping off the island at many points would have you stepping off into the deepest parts of the ocean, literally. For that reason, Jamaica had some of the world's most beautiful, and functional, natural harbors. Cruise ships and other industrial vessels, such as those transporting the aluminum mined in Jamaica, could pull right up to the edge of the island because the bottomless sea was only one step off the land in many places. Even on the beaches where there was sand, often the swimming area was very narrow because the sand would quickly angle down to the ocean floor. Negril was an exception with its white sandy beaches where one could walk far out.

The seas around Jamaica were treacherous and commanded respect, Kurt had always warned her. He'd heard many stories throughout his childhood of swimmers who had risked their lives in areas marked "no swimming/off limits" whose bodies either were never found or whose body parts were recovered badly mangled and mutilated by sharks.

As Maggie looked out into the sea pondering the ocean depths just a few feet away from where she stood surrounded by the prickly, almost desert-like vegetation that continuously stood up to the harsh ocean winds, she felt her shoulders embraced by a strong arm of a tall man standing on her right.

"Are you imagining what it must have been like to be a pirate, Maggie?" he asked.

"I was doing just that," she replied, turning around to face a smiling Bucky, the tall fellow from the Peace Corps who walked with a slight limp.

"There are modern pirates, you know," he responded with a wink.

"Really?"

"Yes, and I think we'll hear about the modern-day pirates when we go to the embassy."

"What do you mean?" Maggie was intrigued.

"I'm talking about some of the island politicians. There is some piracy that occurs whenever the international relief organizations provide aid and money to a small country. The local politicians who traffic-manage the incoming benevolences take their cut — I'm sure they probably consider themselves consultants and think of their 'cut' as a commission. But they skim about ten percent off the top of whatever aid comes in. There's a famous politician on the island called 'Mr. Ten Percent' by the locals."

"How do you know so much about Jamaica?" Maggie asked.

"I've been here before," he smiled. "This will be my fourth rotation in Jamaica," he continued. "I'm beginning to think I'm a Jamaican at heart. I love this island culture. I don't know where I'll be assigned but I'm hoping for Kingston. The Kingstonians are a fun-loving, family-oriented, business-minded lot, and their city is absolutely breathtakingly beautiful at night with those lights shining in the homes that are nestled in the mountains. The Jamaicans are always hustling during the week, but on the week-end they really know how to have a good time. We usually meet up at the Yacht Club near Port Royal and then some of us will take a cruiser out and anchor near one of the cays. Then we'll return in the afternoon and meet back at the Yacht Club in the evening for dinner and dancing to the music of a band with some hot Latin or Calypso singer."

Maggie already knew most of the things he was talking about, but the way he spoke of the island was lyrical and poetic and she enjoyed listening to his affectionate portrait of it.

"What do you do when you work?" Maggie wondered out loud.

He laughed out loud at her bold insinuation. "Believe it or not, I do work, Maggie," he replied, with a boisterous laugh. "But the kind of work I do is enhanced if I have good connections in the local community. I'm a psychologist and I work out of a community shelter, mostly with youth, counseling them about everything from birth control to child abuse to financial management to suicide. Knowing some prominent business people, doctors, and lawyers in Kingston helps me get my job done."

"I can see that," replied Maggie.

"Hey, Maggie! Why don't you go to a party at the Yacht Club with me tonight? I can introduce you to some Kingstonians who can help you with your mission work. I know my way around this city, and I think you'll be impressed at what a Christian country Jamaica is. But then, you probably already know that since your husband spent his boyhood here. I keep forgetting that."

It hadn't occurred to Maggie to bring a cocktail dress with her, so she asked Bucky to take her shopping that afternoon. Luckily, they could walk to dozens of shops near the Courtleigh Manor. Their hotel was very near the Sheraton and its surrounding shopping mecca. Manicured, well-coiffed ladies bustled in and out of the boutiques which offered exquisite garments at exotic prices. Luckily, Maggie found a basic black dress on the sale rack in one of the fancier boutiques. Only a few blocks away in every direction, native Jamaicans lived in tin hovels and zinc shanties and eked out a meager existence based on a lifestyle of bartering, continuous hustling, and tending to their booths in craft markets where business was "feast or famine" depending on whether the cruise ships were in port or tourist buses paid a visit.

Bucky had told the truth. He did seem to have a lot of friends at the Yacht Club, and they seemed intrigued by his pretty, friendly companion. They appeared even more intrigued when Bucky told them Maggie was essentially in Jamaica as a missionary, to aid in the healing and restoration after the hurricane. There was a festive mood in the air, and Maggie felt her body swaying to the beat of the Caribbean rhythms undulating in the tropical warmth of an outdoor party where women in haute couture laughed and chatted around the pool while the men downed rum and Coke and discussed their business problems in the aftermath of Hilda.

Maggie definitely felt like an outsider, although the Jamaicans there went out of their way to welcome her and show her hospitality. It was a society which was very chauvinistic, and that was obvious by the way the socializing occurred. Except for coming together to dance and reconnect briefly in order to freshen a drink, the women and men gravitated into their own spheres, and Maggie didn't belong in either sphere. The planet itself gets to be a small world, as everyone discovers from time to time, but an island is definitely a very small place where it seems "everybody knows everybody" — and "everybody knows everybody's business." At that party of nearly two hundred people, Maggie could easily spot the outsiders. There was a young professional woman from Miami there with her boyfriend whose family had business interests on the island. She was a petite, attractive lady but she had little in common with the affluent wives discussing their latest problems related to the reliability of domestic help since the hurricane struck. These Jamaican women, and the other wives imported by their husbands from islands like Barbados and Trinidad, had a lifestyle that looked somewhat appealing to Maggie, a professional woman from a hustle-bustle culture where women were hardly ever pampered, seldom had time for manicures and pedicures, and unceasingly had to shoulder at least half of the responsibility for making the money for their families. From the outside looking in, the lives of these Jamaican women appeared free of the cares and duty and responsibility that weighted down professional American women.

The women were nice to Maggie, apparently out of their affection for Bucky, whom they seem to have more or less "adopted." One by one, several of the women shared with Maggie their own stories of how they had found their way to the Baptist faith or

Methodist religion which many of them seemed to practice. Except for the women who had grown up on nearby islands like Cuba or the Cayman Islands or others, the women told stories of British relatives who decades ago had settled in Jamaica. Those Brits had named Jamaica's three counties Cornwall, Middlesex, and Surrey, after counties in England.

"Don't think everyone in Jamaica has British ancestors, Maggie," said Bucky, as he came to her side to escort her to the hors d'oeuvres. "You can see that a lot of the food at this party is Lebanese and Syrian. There's tabouli right there next to the French pastries created by some of Jamaica's famous chefs. This is a funny old island, Maggie, where deep pockets of other cultures still exist, untouched by time or tourists. Have you ever heard of Germantown? That's a fascinating place off the beaten track up from Negril that's still a pocket of German culture. It's like a culture warp going there, because you'll see gorgeous blond, aristocratic-looking Teutonic women and children who speak the island patois just like the poor black Jamaicans they have lived beside and intermingled with while maintaining their cultural markings. And then there's cockpit country, where on most published maps you'll see its motto described as 'me no sen, you no come.' That's an aggressive warning that visitors aren't welcome there, and it's thought that the antisocial Maroons who inhabit cockpit country are the descendants of some black African slaves brought to Jamaica who were extracted from some of Africa's fiercest and most warrior-like tribes."

He paused suddenly and a different-looking smile came over his face. He was looking at her as a man looks at a woman. Peering down from his 6' 3" frame, his eyes deliberately and slowly looked her over from head to toe. He smiled again, this time a broader and more mischievous smile.

"You don't look like a missionary, Maggie," he chided.

"Why can't a missionary look like a woman?" she countered.

"I love the way you look, Maggie, but it's just that one doesn't expect a minister to be trim and beautiful and have curves like a real girl! Don't look now, but I think those women over there in the corner looking at you are discussing just that. They probably find it incredible that you are a minister looking so chic in your sophisticated, sexy black dress with spaghetti straps."

Maggie took a sip of her drink and didn't respond for a moment. She had certainly heard that familiar complaint that she didn't "look like a minister."

Suddenly the beat of the Reggae music vibrations in the tropical evening air captured her attention as she heard the lyrics of a familiar song. One of the things Kurt had taken with him from Jamaica was an affection for Bob Marley's Reggae sound, so "the beat," as Kurt referred to Reggae, was often heard in the Dillitz house. She felt instantly connected to Kurt and the children just listening to the lyrics:

Don't worry, 'bout a 'ting,
Cause every little 'ting's
Gonna be alright.
Saying, don't worry, 'bout a 'ting,
Cause every little 'ting's
Gonna be alright.

The sounds of Reggae were soothing to the soul. Marley's Reggae made Maggie remember what Kurt had told her about the "Jamaica white" skin color of many of the island's natives and then about the many conversations they'd had when he taught her about this island culture. The locals used the term "Jamaica white" to refer to a person of interracial descent, a person whose skin looked white at first glance but whose relatives included the Africans imported to the island for slavery. Jamaica continued to be an island where the culture was a mix of half-remembered African traditions mingled with the customs of the British. Reggae music was a product of that culture. Reggae itself was a mix of the New Orleans rhythm and blues broadcast by American radio stations with ska music, the "hot-beat" dance floor music that was so popular when Marley was writing songs.

The rock-and-roll music called Reggae finally cracked the American charts with the song "Rastaman Vibration." Marley became an international celebrity with the same song that also endeared him to ghetto youth worldwide. Youth international looked up to this boy who himself was from the ghetto. Marley had lived as a teenager in the most notorious shantytown in Kingston called Trench Town, so called because it was constructed over a ditch that drained the sewage of Old Kingston.

Just as Marley's influence was spreading all over the world, a virulent cancer that had begun with a neglected toe was spreading all over Marley's body. At thirty-six years old, he died at the height of his popularity and his body was taken to his birthplace at Nine Mile, a hamlet in the rural, mountainous Jamaican surroundings of St. Ann to the north of the island.

In every way Marley's life had been representative of Jamaican culture. Marley's mother was an eighteen-year-old black girl who coupled with a fifty-year-old white quartermaster with the British West Indian Regiment. Although the couple married after Bob was born and produced another child, the white family of Bob's father applied such pressure that the couple split up and the British captain seldom saw his son, although he provided financial support for the boy who would become the first superstar from the Third World.

Marley's music began to change and focus on more spiritual and social issues as he embraced Rastafarianism. In his search for the meaning of life, the young Marley met a shrewd Jamaican preacher named Marcus Garvey. Garvey had popularized the notion that a black king would come who would deliver the Negro race from white domination. Jamaican followers of the black preacher decided that the man crowned the two hundred and twenty-fifth Emperor of Ethiopia — a man named Ras Tafari Makonnen who preferred to be called Haile Selassie — was the redeemer of the Negro race whom the black preacher had promised. The new religion found a devout Rastafarian in Bob Marley. Marley was rejecting the gang world that could have seduced him in favor of the benevolent community of the Rasta faith. As a devout Rasta, Marley believed his brethren to be from the Lost Tribe of Israel, and many of Marley's melodies expressed the thirst for spiritual freedom.

So it was an irony that the "sufferahs" in the shantytown of West Kingston were the ones who turned on Marley. Ghetto youth worldwide were tuning in and turning on to his firm Rastafarian stance, but that popularity didn't please the ghetto gang lords. When Marley announced that he would hold a free concert in Kingston's national Heroes Park to stress the need for peace in the city's slums, the warring gangs in the business of turmoil and murder took offense.

Marley's proposed free concert came on the eve of a government election. The political turmoil preceding the election was the catalyst for increased gang violence, and some of that violence was directed at Marley. On the eve of his concert, gunmen broke into Marley's house and shot him. Badly wounded by his would-be assassins, he decided to leave Jamaica for London, but not before he came on stage on the scheduled day of the concert to play a free set in defiance of the gang lords.

An arm around her waist jolted Maggie

back to reality. She turned her face upwards towards Bucky's smiling face.

"Time to go home, partner," he whispered.

A chauffeur-driven limousine waiting outside whisked them from the Yacht Club and down the narrow nine-mile strip of road that led from the Port Royal area to the mainland island. Looking at the homes twinkling in the Jamaican mountains, Maggie felt overwhelmed by the beauty of this mountainous island that was geologically a rock jutting to unfathomable depths beneath them. Suddenly she became aware of how fragile she felt on this long, lonely stretch of two-lane highway that seemed so boldly out of place in the middle of the ocean. Her thoughts raced to Kurt and the kids. How she missed them. It would be more than a week before she'd see them.

Bucky walked her back to her hotel room at the Courtleigh Manor and said goodnight. When Maggie walked into her room, she saw a telephone message. Her heart jumped! Kurt had called! But the message, when she turned it over, was from Dr. Farmer:

> PLEASE CALL ME IMMEDIATELY AFTER YOU RETURN.
>
> BILL FARMER

"Dr. Farmer?" she asked of the voice that

answered the phone.

"Yes, Maggie," he replied, recognizing her voice instantly. "You've been out late, haven't you?" The tone was friendly but there was a touch of condescension and reprimand.

"Yes, I met some nice Jamaicans."

"I'm sure you did, but I need to talk with you about some things tonight."

"Tonight?"

"Yes, well, I had thought we could do it earlier but I didn't realize you were going to a party."

She didn't feel like having any business meeting at ten o'clock at night, but there didn't seem to be an easy way out of it. A headache probably wouldn't work.

Even though he said he'd be right over after she agreed to meet with him, Maggie didn't dream he would be on her doorstep within two minutes.

"Maggie, you look very nice," he gushed when she opened the door. After she made them some coffee, Maggie kicked off her shoes and climbed onto the couch, sliding her stockinged legs under her. She hadn't had time to change so she still wore the black cocktail dress she'd worn to the party.

Maggie kept waiting for the business discussion to begin but he seemed intent on engaging her in conversation about music and books and graduate school trivia. The conversation would have been interesting enough on another day, but at the moment she felt tired and homesick for her children and Kurt.

Suddenly, all the lights went out.

"Oh, no, another blackout," groaned Dr. Farmer. "That's been happening all night," said his voice from the pitch black darkness. "In these circumstances, and from now on, you'll have to call me Bill."

"OK, Bill, but I think we might want to call it an evening since we really can't work."

She heard him slide onto the couch where she was sitting and then, without a word, she felt one of his hands reaching between her legs and the other pulling down one of the straps of her dress, exposing her breasts. Then she felt his wet mouth on hers as his hands continued to explore and paw her. He was pulling down her pantyhose and trying to take off her dress.

"Bill, what are you doing?"

He didn't stop or answer. In fact, he pushed her down on the couch and pinned her chest and arms against his massive torso as he tried to unlock and straighten her legs to make it easier to pull down her panties. She was strong, but he was bigger and stronger.

"Stop it! No!" Maggie whispered, trying not to create a scene that would wake up the Peace Corps duo sleeping in the next suite. She felt overpowered by his large frame and intimidated by his aggressiveness.

"Take it easy, darling," he said, as he pawed her.

The next few minutes seemed like a long time. Finally, Maggie managed to pull herself away and just as she plopped into the chair near the couch, the lights suddenly reappeared and she saw her body exposed in what then seemed a tacky and seedy hotel environment. She looked, and felt, like a two-bit prostitute. She was repulsed by the sight of herself. Her breasts were hanging out of her dress and her pantyhose were around her knees. His clothes were on but he had gotten as far as unzipping his pants so they clung loosely to his hips. She blinked to focus her eyes in the gaudy electric haze which had probably been produced by an emergency power generator.

"Oh, Maggie, I'm sorry, I don't know what got into me," Bill apologized profusely. "I hope I didn't offend you. Let me help you put your beautiful self back together, darling," he said, approaching her chair. The sight of him enraged and scared her. *What if the power went out again?*

"No. Please, just go," she said in a tone of reserved anger.

Before she could pull her dress up completely, she felt his hand pulling up her right strap and caressing her breast as he pretended to help. She pulled her body away angrily.

"You have a wonderful body, Maggie," he whispered softly. She turned her back on him and marched to the door where, seconds later, he joined her. She did not look at him as he came toward her and stood at the door.

"I don't know what got into me, darling," he began, in a contrite tone that sounded very practiced and professional. "I just find you so sexually appealing, and we're so far from home and from our responsibilities."

"But not from our principles and our values. Dr. Farmer, please leave," was all she could say.

Once she shut the door behind him, she broke out crying, as though a sudden drenching rain had come along. It was a cry of relief more than anything else. She felt safe again, sort of. *But what was that all about? What had she done or said to arouse that kind of emotion? What was happening here?*

While she was getting ready for bed, Maggie felt an overpowering rush of helplessness, combined with a cheapened sense of self worth. *How could she ever tell Kurt? She wanted to call him now, but how could she call him long distance to tell him that the senior minister had tried to rape and fondle her? The incident was, mercifully, over. It didn't seem fair to call him long distance to worry him. She couldn't do that to him.*

She could hardly sleep even when she got into bed. She got up a couple of times to make sure the door was locked. It was. Thank God.

The next morning she put on her bathing suit for a morning swim and went out by the pool near the restaurant. Bucky and most of the others in the Peace Corps group were there.

"What's the matter with you?" Bucky noticed immediately her fidgety and downcast mood.

"Nothing. I just didn't sleep well last night."

The word was passed around that minibuses would be available in front of the Courtleigh Manor at twelve noon to take the Americans to the U.S. Embassy for the beginning of their briefing. Maggie felt like a robot going through the motions. The purity of all this was suddenly gone. Something that had seemed appetizing and sweet had a rank and putrid odor. The gorgeous Caribbean sun was a tranquilizer for any malady of the mind, but Maggie couldn't shake off the dread she felt at seeing Dr. Farmer again.

She did see him again soon. They exchanged pleasantries, as though nothing had happened, when they met outside the hotel at noon to catch the minibus. On the bus, Maggie sat with a woman psychologist from the Peace Corps. Once they were at the embassy, she and Farmer sat with different groups. Maggie sat with Bucky and other Peace Corps acquaintances while Dr. Farmer gravitated toward the few other senior ministers who were there.

At the end of the second day of their briefing, they were going to receive their assignment. When the announcement was made the next day that Maggie Dillitz and Bill Farmer were assigned to Ocho Rios to help a major tourist city get back to normal, Maggie's first reaction was fright. She felt nervous about breaking away from the group on assignment for a week with Dr. Farmer. Bucky would be leaving tomorrow for Port Antonio, a city at considerable distance from "Ochy," as the locals referred to Ocho Rios.

That night, after dinner at the restaurant, Maggie and Bucky split from the other

Peace Corps volunteers to take a walk towards the Sheraton. Maybe it was the way he put his arm around her as they walked; maybe it was the thought that she would possibly never see him again after tomorrow morning; maybe it was just her great need to tell someone about what had begun to seem like a dirty secret, but she told him she wanted to tell him something. And then she told him everything.

Bucky was visibly shocked and offended and outraged. The city streets were fairly quiet and well lit as they walked through a chic tourist section.

"You've got to report him, Maggie."

"Bucky, I can't report what happened. My career is on thin ice as it is. It would just be my credibility against his credibility, and there would be no contest. In a way, even this trip is a 'quick fix' for my career."

"Some fix," he sneered. "Maggie, he's using you. He's taking advantage of you when you're obviously vulnerable. You're not a child, and you have a responsibility to report him."

"Responsibility? I know I have responsibility, Bucky. That's what my whole life is about — duty and responsibility. But my main responsibility is to my family, and there wouldn't be any good result for them if my career fell apart and I lost my job in some tawdry scandal. My husband is struggling in the construction business right now, and I just can't put any more pressure on him."

"You're a hostage, Maggie. That's what sexual abuse does. It imprisons the victim. And I don't like your going to Ocho Rios for a week with that dirty old man. Do you think you'll be alright?"

"I'll be OK, Bucky. But just knowing that you know somehow helps. I can't burden Kurt with this; he's just got too many business worries and general aggravations at the moment. He sacrificed a lot career-wise so that I could go into ministry, and I can't just allow all our hard work to come to naught."

"OK, then don't tell Kurt now. I'm not talking about whether you tell Kurt or not. You're turning the main decision here into a subset of the decision. You should confront Farmer with this, you should notify his superiors, and you should not go to Ocho Rios with him."

"How can you be so judgmental about my decision not to tell? I have thought this out, Bucky. What happened, happened in a hotel room late at night when only the two of us were there. I'm a rookie in my profession and he's a respected veteran and 'man of the cloth.' Who do you think would be believed?

Just be practical. I don't want to fight a losing battle, can't you understand that without thinking that I'm copping out on my responsibility? I see responsibility in every direction I turn, and I surely think I am making this decision with an attitude of responsibility toward my family. I can't afford to be out of a job, Bucky. I changed career fields when I moved into ministry, and I don't have a lot of flexibility and mobility at middle age. I have to make this work, and I have to make it work in spite of some bumps in the road."

"How can this work for you, Maggie? How can you imagine that you can just go on about your business as though this didn't happen? This harassment isn't going to go away. It's only going to get worse."

"Maybe I shouldn't have invited him into my room. Maybe I shouldn't have been wearing what you implied yourself was a provocative dress. I don't know, I just don't want to talk about it anymore. I want it to be over. Now, can we just enjoy this last evening in Kingston?"

They spent the next half hour meandering the well-lit city blocks near the Sheraton. They were approached several times by Jamaicans hustling ganja.

"Looking for some smoke?" was the typical way they were approached by salesmen of "the weed," or marijuana.

Aside from several offers of weed, Maggie and Bucky were not disturbed. Back at the Courtleigh Manor, they had a tropical fruit punch drink near the pool and lingered there, not wanting to end the evening because they both knew this leavetaking would be their last. Maggie would leave for her week's stay in Ocho Rios the following day with Dr. Farmer, Bucky would leave for his yearlong assignment in Port Antonio, and it seemed unlikely that their paths would cross again. There was a strong animal magnetism between them, the kind of magnetism that was like a strong natural force, not like a contrived attraction created by seduction and gamesmanship. Maggie knew she would miss this tall, handsome, spiritual man with a pronounced limp.

"How'd you get that limp, anyway, Bucky?" she finally asked.

"I thought you'd never ask!" he teased her. "It's not a glamorous tale, Maggie. I got run over by a car when I was a teenager. I was on my way to college with a basketball scholarship — I'm nearly 6' 4" — but that ended after the wreck. Luckily, like He always does, God used something bad to make something good, and I found a deeper spirituality inside myself once the accident slowed me down."

"God can always help us use the bad things for good, can't He?" Maggie smiled as she responded. She appreciated this gentle, sensitive, kindhearted messenger from God. It was people like Bucky who illustrated that maternal instincts did not belong only to women.

They clasped hands as Bucky walked her back to her apartment at the Courtleigh. He bent his tall frame down like a giraffe to plant a lingering kiss on her forehead. She stood there feeling like somebody's very special kid sister. They hugged and promised to keep in touch. Then Maggie went inside and closed the door behind her, certain she'd never see Bucky again.

OCHO RIOS

The next morning was rushed. She threw her belongings into her two suitcases and met Dr. Farmer at the front desk at eight o'clock to check out. After a quick breakfast of coffee, fruit, and toast, they were whisked by taxi to another location where they boarded a minibus.

The trip over the mountains from Kingston to Ocho Rios took about five hours, and it was a beautiful ride. Smiling school boys in khaki shirts and blue shorts and girls in blue skirts with white shirts walked beside the road during lunchtime, as did women walking erect carrying baskets of clothes and groceries on their heads.

Men carrying machetes as they walked along the side of the road were a reminder that Jamaica was a jungle, and that immediately off the road were thousands of paths, many of them created by the Arawak Indians hundreds of years ago, which had to be continuously tamed by the sharp blades of the swordlike, razor-sharp machete. Maggie saw the machete in action when the minivan stopped by one of the many roadside stands they passed selling pineapples, sugar cane, coconuts, bananas, and Jamaican otahete apples. Maggie sipped the juice from a coconut shell through a straw. Then the lithe, beautiful Jamaican vendor took the coconut and, in two deft blows, cut the coconut shell away so Maggie could eat the meat. Maggie stared at the beautiful Jamaican girl as she worked. She was thin, as were most Jamaicans, and her tawny skin color implied many years of genetic mixing among people of African, German, Spanish, and English descent. She had large, expressive eyes and gorgeous full lips. She could not have been more than nineteen years old. In an industrialized country, she could have landed a job as a model.

Maggie found herself wondering about the ironies and apparent unfairnesses of fate as she stared at this pretty young woman intensely involved in her work. What made sense about life's being a Russian roulette game in so many ways? How fair was it that a beautiful young black girl born in the Bronx, New York, had a chance to become a model while her twin, born in a tropical paradise where unemployment was rampant, had a chance to operate a roadside stand and marry a man who himself had few prospects for employment? Was there an equity here that Maggie couldn't see or comprehend?

She felt impertinent wondering how God Himself could view with grace such a world where so many inequalities and inequities existed.

Just as Maggie was paying, a young child of four years old ran from the bushes and grabbed hold of the young girl's skirt. After the girl made change, she reached down to gently pat the child on his back, and Maggie saw in the happy faces of this mother and child a richness and a serenity that made Maggie stop thinking about unfairness and poverty. Poverty was not the right thought to have about Jamaica, anyway. Jamaica was poor, but even the poorest folks could eke out a meager existence and live on the natural foodstuffs and fishing. This supposedly "third-world" island seemed to have so much more intelligence in the way in which it had virtually eliminated the extremes of poverty that ran rampant in the industrialized countries. Perhaps Jamaica did not need a major dose of the kind of "progress" and "civilization" the industrialized countries stood for.

They passed out of the heavy mountainous country and, as they passed through Moneague, it was clear they were on a descent from the mountains and in transition from simple mountain living to the hustle and bustle of a big city with a booming tourist trade. As they rode through Fern Gully, Maggie marveled at the panoramic view of the mountains with oversized ferns everywhere. The roadside stands in Fern Gully offered not fruit but wood carvings made from the Jamaican hardwood tree, the lignum vitae, or "the tree of life," as the Jamaicans called it. The driver of the minibus yelled out that he could not stop because there were few good places for a large vehicle to pull off the road, but he urged them to find their way back to Fern Gully by taxi to examine the straw baskets, handbags, and carryalls as well as the wooden animal carvings. Fern Gully was famous for such creations, he told them, and they should visit the craft booths there. The hungry vendors would welcome the sight of a tourist, he said.

At the foot of Fern Gully, their descent from the mountains was suddenly over and they were on the coast. After a quick turn around a roundabout, they were on a road which led to the sea. Maggie moved around in her seat to catch a glimpse of the cruise ship docked at the edge of the road. The minivan turned into a hotel at the entrance of which were two uniformed guards who scrutinized them before signaling the driver to enter the parking lot of the hotel. As soon as they drove in, they saw a few people who looked like businessmen speaking German. Maggie also saw Jamaican women in pink uniforms who appeared to be hotel employees. The sign on the hotel entrance read "Fisherman's Point."

Dr. Farmer explained to Maggie as they were checking in that a prominent and wealthy Jamaican family in the bauxite business had donated the use of their three-bedroom apartment during this mission project. Apparently the family that owned the condo lived in Kingston and sometimes rented out the condo through the condominium association, but the recent hurricane had effectively nearly rid the island of tourists, except for the most adventurous. Whatever the reason, philanthropy and generosity or a less well-motivated impulse, an expensively decorated and handsomely furnished apartment was put at the disposal of Maggie and Dr. Farmer through the coordinated efforts of Methodist churches in Kingston and Ocho Rios. The smiling, uniformed maid and bellboy who showed Maggie and Dr. Farmer to apartment 47C were surprised to learn that Maggie was a minister just like Dr. Farmer.

The bellboy recommended that Maggie take the bedroom on the second floor. He set her bags on the carpet and then opened the French doors that led out to a small patio overlooking a spectacular bay where, during regular tourist season, he told her, motor boats and jet skis put on a show for the sunbathers relaxing on the white sandy beach.

The maid and bellboy then settled Dr. Farmer into the bedroom on the third floor.

After spending a few moments putting her underwear in the dresser drawers and hanging her dresses in the closet, Maggie went downstairs to the first floor where the kitchen, living room, and dining room were. She found Dr. Farmer in the kitchen receiving instructions from the maid and bellboy on how the appliances worked and what services the staff would be providing.

After Roy, the bellboy, and Olympia, the maid, had gone, Maggie and Dr. Farmer were left alone.

"We don't start work until this evening when we have dinner with some missionaries, Maggie," Dr. Farmer said. "Why don't we go down by the pool to relax?" He sounded friendly, almost like a schoolboy, and looked harmless, as though the incident in Kingston had never occurred.

She thought about it. *Perhaps I should let bygones be bygones, let the past be the past. Isn't that what Christians are supposed to do?*

"I don't know . . . ummm . . . I might do some reading . . . and I need to call home."

"Oh, it's way too expensive to call home this time of day. You really should call later. During business hours it's just prohibitive to call overseas, and it's easier to get a connection at night. You can nap in the sun, anyway."

"Well, alright," Maggie replied.

"I'll meet you out by the pool, then," he said, and then he climbed the stairs to his third-floor bedroom.

In her bedroom, Maggie decided against the two-piece bathing suit. It was skimpier than she felt comfortable with. She decided to wear the one-piece black matronly one. It was kind of plain and old fashioned looking. Basically, it was just a tank suit with a soft bra inside it.

She joined Dr. Farmer by the pool and plopped down in the chaise lounge next to him. Ah, the day was beautiful and the sun did feel so good, and she was glad to have a couple of hours to luxuriate beside the pool on this balmy tropical day. She decided to lie on her stomach and take a nap.

A few moments after she had drifted off to a superficial sleep, she felt two hands rubbing oil on her shoulders. She made a quick startled movement, and then she heard Dr. Farmer's voice.

"Don't worry, dear, I'm just going to put some of this sun protector on your skin. This tropical sun can burn you within minutes, you know."

He massaged the lotion into her shoulders, then he took each one of her arms and massaged lotion all over them. Next she felt his hands on the back of her thighs, rubbing the lotion on her legs. His hands moved between her thighs and she felt his fingers on her crotch. She had been almost lulled to sleep by his massage of her shoulders, and then the touch of his fingers on her private parts felt like someone throwing cold water on her. She felt violated. She might have thought that his touch was an accident except that he kept stroking her there. Maggie was mortified and her body stiffened, but she was conscious of not wanting to make a scene. There were about half a dozen people lounging around the pool, most of whom looked like Jamaicans on holiday at their country condo for a few days, and they no doubt would have thought Maggie and Dr. Farmer to be a married couple.

Without jerking wildly or saying a word, she lifted her stiffened torso up by her arms and began to turn around.

"Now if you want me to do the front, Maggie, we'll have to go inside," he whispered in an evil tone with a lecherous stare at her bosom. He wasn't smiling. He was simply staring at her breasts as she tried to sit up in the chaise lounge.

"You are beautiful, dear," he said, with his eyes fixated on her bosom.

"Excuse me, Bill," she finally said, without any emotion in her voice. "I'm going to do a little sightseeing."

"I'll come with you," he volunteered stupidly.

"No," she replied flatly but emphatically, "I'm going alone. I'm going to walk into town and find the craft market to buy my kids some things."

Back in the condo, she quickly threw a casual summer dress on over her bathing suit and put on tennis shoes. One of the laundry workers named Venus gave her directions to the craft market and, once she was outside the protected compound of Fisherman's Point, she felt safe. What an irony. She was supposed to feel safe inside that luxurious tropical haven with guards posted at every entrance to keep the "riff raff" out. Instead, she felt safer amongst the hustlers and street vendors waiting just outside the compound to pounce on the tourists.

"Taxi, mi lady?" . . . "Hey, sweet lady, want your hair braided?" . . . "You want some smoke, honey?" . . . "Hey, lady, will you take a look at my paintings?" Numbed by Farmer's unwelcome advances, Maggie walked past the street hustlers in a daze, past multiple vendors all trying to make a living by selling something to the very few tourists on the island now.

At the craft market, only half the booths were open. Maggie felt herself drawn to one booth where an artist was selling his paintings of Jamaican life in small villages. They struck up a conversation and after forty-five minutes of talking with this man called Oliver about his children and grandchildren, and then about her husband and children, Maggie felt thoroughly homesick. She bought a small painting for Kurt and then she found wooden carved animals — lions, elephants, pigs, rabbits, cats, giraffes — for the children. The craft market was only a twenty-minute walk from Fisherman's Point, and Maggie found herself dragging out this shopping trip just to avoid going back to the condo. But she finally did walk slowly back.

There was a note on the kitchen table with her name on it when she walked upstairs. It was a note from Dr. Farmer stating that he would be beside the pool, dressed for dinner, at six o'clock so that they could be picked up by the O'Connells. The condominium seemed an oppressive place, and she dressed quickly and joined him at the pool. She and Dr. Farmer made small talk until the O'Connells arrived.

The O'Connells were missionaries from Japan who happened to be visiting Jamaica when Hilda struck. They had quickly contacted the mission board to get special permission to stay in the country for a while to assist in the disaster relief. Sally and Edgar O'Connell drove them to a Japanese restaurant in Ocho Rios that was rated "five stars." It was also one of the few restaurants in full operation after the hurricane. When the maitre d' learned that the four of them were in Jamaica on missionary work, he was kind enough to tell them that the restaurant would cover half their meal cost that evening. That proved to be a gracious beginning to a wonderful evening.

With Sally O'Connell, Maggie had an opportunity to talk about motherhood and her children. Sally told her that she and Edgar had met when they were in college. Edgar had fallen into Sally's arms as a friend seeking sympathy for the unrequited love he had felt toward another classmate. Sally said that, at first, she had tried playing matchmaker between Edgar and his would-be girlfriend, but very quickly Sally had discovered that she didn't want to help Edgar hook up with anyone else. Both she and Edgar had nurtured since their childhoods a dream of becoming missionaries, but they didn't share their secret dreams with each other until Edgar was nearing graduation from seminary and they were making plans to marry. Their dreams had been approved by the mission board twenty-five years ago, and then they spent their honeymoon and the next two and a half decades in Japan. The two biological children they bore and the two Japanese children they adopted were grown now, Sally told Maggie, and she was enjoying a new kind of married life with her husband and childhood sweetheart. That's why they were in Jamaica, Sally told Maggie. They were implementing a plan they'd made to visit at least one country a year, if their finances could afford it.

The O'Connells were well connected into the relief organizations serving the island, and a plan was made at dinner that night that Maggie and Sally would spend their days together helping to distribute the food airlifted in from other countries and to monitor the temporarily homeless now sleeping in gigantic tents erected by American military forces in several of the parks and wide open spaces in Ocho Rios. According to the plan, Edgar O'Connell and Bill Farmer would work on the cleanup teams on the stretches of highway near the ocean around Ochy. Maggie was so relieved that she would not be spending the days with Farmer. But she dreaded the nights in that condominium, just knowing that he would be there.

After the O'Connells dropped Maggie and Farmer back at Fisherman's Point in a rental car donated to them during their stay by Island Rentals, Maggie realized how weary of traveling she was and how homesick for Kurt and the kids she was becoming. Dr. Farmer insisted that she have a glass of water or cup of tea before bedtime so they could plan their week's agenda. But Maggie was in no mood to be pushed or bullied or bossed around. And she would not allow herself to be seduced again by the concept of forgiveness.

"I'm going straight to bed," she announced defiantly, with an undisguised unfriendly tone in her voice.

"Don't forget," he replied, in a tone of voice that contained arrogance and condescension, "you are here on business, and if there is business still to do, you must postpone your pillow talk."

Maggie felt her emotions welling up and she knew she could not hold her tongue.

"Perhaps it's monkey business you think needs to be done, Dr. Farmer, but you will need to do it by yourself. I'm going to bed." She refused, she vowed to herself, to ever call him Bill.

"You are certainly behaving in a rather careless professional manner, my dear, considering that your rather rocky career so far in the ministry could use a few friends in high places."

"You may be right, sir, and I appreciate your opinion, but I'm tired and I'm going to bed. Good night."

After she locked her door and climbed into bed, she knew she had blown it. She knew objectively that she should have "kept her cool" and not insulted him, but her emotions had gotten the best of her. It was so disgusting to watch him prey upon her — yes, watch him. That's the way Maggie felt, as though she were on the outside of some surreal dream observing the two characters. Even now, as she lay down, she felt as though she'd spoken out of turn somehow.

The next six days were exhausting and exhilarating. Every morning at a quarter past six, the O'Connells would pick Maggie and

Bill up at Fisherman's Point. Then the men would drop the ladies off near the town center so that they could spend the day ministering to the helpless, homeless, and hungry. The men would then drive to a different point each day to participate in directing the work crews that were cleaning debris such as limbs and branches and sometimes nearly whole trees off the road.

Water was one of the main problems after the hurricane.

"It's interesting how God brings us right back to the basics, isn't it, Maggie?" Sally would frequently ask. Maggie loved those days of working with Sally. She was a kind-hearted soul who always had a smile on her face, and she radiated the love of Christ in everything she did. Watching Sally was like watching a sermon in action. The Apostle Paul had instructed Christians of his day to "be little Christs," to let the nature of Christ so overpower and transform their nature that they would become "little Christs." In watching so many of Sally's gestures and actions, Maggie would suddenly connect with a piece of scripture that had seemed more academic and theoretical before she saw Sally implementing scripture. Scripture in action, that's how she thought of Sally.

"I'd rather see a sermon than hear one any

day," Maggie said to Sally suddenly at mid-day on the third day they were working together. "Who was the poet who penned those words?"

"It was Edgar A. Guest, darling. The poem is called *Sermons We See* and I've read it aloud to students many times. It's a lovely poem."

"Those are the words I think of when I think of you, Sally."

As Sally's brilliant blue eyes turned to stare into Maggie's, she saw Sally blush just before Sally reached over to embrace her.

"Thank you, dear, for saying such a sweet thing. You're *my* inspiration, though. I miss my children so much and you seem as though you could be one of them. I feel very much stronger because you are at my side during these days."

Maggie found herself comparing this positive, energetic woman to her own domineering, meddlesome mother. After the cold, imperious treatment she'd received from her mother throughout her life, Maggie had had trouble forming friendships with other women in her teenage years. She'd been trained to think of female relationships as being essentially mercurial and difficult and emotionally unsatisfying. Just how deeply scarred Maggie had been by her mother became clear when Maggie was pregnant with her daughter. After a sonogram had revealed that she was carrying a girl, Maggie had worried privately during her daily walks that she and her then-unborn child would one day have a relationship of hostility, too, just as Maggie had with her mother. After Ashley was born, Maggie learned to trust her ability to mother and love a daughter but, deep inside, at terrible crossroads in her life, Maggie feared that one day she would be just like the bitchy, hard woman who had raised her. But in this woman Sally, Maggie saw what her grandmother had often told her — that a mother's love is close to the saviour's love. Maggie felt herself getting stronger around this fine lady who was now, in Maggie's mind, the picture of what a Christian mother should be.

There were two days left before Maggie and Dr. Farmer's departure from Ocho Rios to Montego Bay and then home. It seemed that the opportunity to talk intimately with Sally came out of the blue. It was about half past four when a message arrived from one of the work crew members going home that the men would be working late and the ladies should walk the half mile back to Fisherman's Point, have dinner, and wait for them. They would likely be quite late, the messenger said.

The ladies arrived back at Fisherman's Point at nearly dusk, then decided to shower and have a bite at Mike's On The Bay, the restaurant downstairs. Once they were at dinner, Maggie knew she would have to confide in this special person whom she'd come to regard as almost a saint.

"Sally, I have to tell you something," was how Maggie began, and then she recounted nearly every humiliating detail of Dr. Farmer's sexual advances. Sally never interrupted once and showed no emotion. She just listened. Finally, when Maggie stopped talking, Sally spoke.

"Is that all, Maggie? Is that everything? Have you told me everything?"

"Yes."

"You poor darling. That's a horrible and degrading thing you've had to put up with. And I heard you imply that you felt somehow responsible for arousing him. That's inappropriate, Maggie, to accept any of the responsibility for his actions. What Farmer has done to you has very little to do with his being aroused. It has to do primarily with being in a position of power and authority. Farmer's sexual harassment of you is just a means by which he can exert power over you and he's using his access to the 'good ole' boy' network to implement his control of you. I think he must feel very threatened by you, somehow, so if he gains control over your body, he probably thinks he won't feel threatened anymore. That's what he probably imagines, anyway. But what you must realize, my dear, is that his sexual aggression toward you is essentially a hostile act, and it's a 'no win-no win' situation for you. You have told me that you feel responsible somehow. Maybe you're too pretty, or too sensual, or wore the wrong thing, but you're doing what women almost always do in this situation. Most victims just suffer in silence because they blame themselves and tend to think they brought it on themselves."

Sally paused, and Maggie remained in an intent state, staring at this woman whom she respected greatly. Then Sally continued.

"I have talked with some women in Japan about this same subject, Maggie. The women pioneers entering professional life are experiencing the same kind of discrimination, and it *is* a form of discrimination. There seems to be a hostile attitude among some men about women being in the work place at all, and so many professional men have taken the view, 'Well, if you women want to be here, then you're going to take whatever we dish out.' And some men will do this if they think they can get away with it. Dr. Farmer is very smart. He realizes what a compromising situation you're in. After the Amos sermon you told me about, there are many people who would choose to question your judgement. So he rides in as your white knight, and then your white knight tries to prey on you and take advantage of you behind closed doors, where it's just your word against his in the unlikely event that you have the nerve to go public with this. It just shows you, Maggie. Even in the highest and most intellectual arenas, sexism persists, because it is about power and domination. Educated people in high places are just smarter and can hide it more easily, but it is about power and control."

"What should I do?" Maggie trusted this strong, kind woman. She might not follow her advice, but she still wanted to hear it.

"I'm not sure, honey. You're in a tough spot. It angers me very much, but I can't let the anger blind me to my objective view of what's happening here. Basically Farmer is doing this because he thinks he can get away with it, and what I have observed in Japan is that wherever sexual discrimination is flagrant, management has permitted it to happen. Farmer is counting on people having a low opinion of you, a high opinion of him, and he's probably counting on a fairly permissive or at least understanding attitude by the men in positions higher than his. He's got you in a very tough spot, that's for sure. You could look like a promiscuous woman if you tell, and you could appear to be a promiscuous woman if you don't tell. That's what's going on in his mind, I think."

Maggie felt shocked. She liked Sally, but she hadn't expected such lucid reasoning and practical analysis from this plainspoken and refined woman.

"I think you need someone to argue your case," Sally continued.

"I can't go through any legal battle, Sally. I don't have the stomach for it now, and I don't want to put my husband and children through it."

"I'm not talking about lawyers and courtrooms, Maggie. A lawsuit is a very imperfect way of achieving social justice in a case like this. You'd be an object of curiosity thrust into the limelight more than you care to be, and even if you won the lawsuit, the judge won't be there later on in the workplace when you're dealing with the unbearably reactionary behavior of him and other colleagues."

"What can I do, then?"

"I'm going to intercede for you, Maggie.

I'm going to let Farmer know that I know his little secret, and I'm going to let him know that it's no longer a secret."

"I don't know . . ." Maggie protested weakly.

"This is the best way, my dear, trust me. You'll be reluctant to report this to anyone since Farmer is your boss, and we both know you might not get a sympathetic ear anyway. Trust me, Maggie. Making sure it's not a secret is the key to making sure you don't have to put up with it anymore. Farmer won't want to make an enemy out of me, Maggie. Edgar and I have spent a long and distinguished career in ministry, and my word would be trusted totally if I ever spoke a word against him." She smiled and reached across the table to pat Maggie gently on the hand, reassuringly. "Mother Teresa doesn't have a better reputation than I do, dear; she's just a little better known. So I'm going to use my good reputation as a potential weapon against him."

Maggie and Sally were eating their salads when Bill Farmer and Edgar O'Connell arrived at the restaurant. The men had showered, it appeared, and Farmer had loaned Edgar a clean shirt that was too large for his tall, thin frame. The four of them exchanged pleasantries and shared their experiences from the day as they savored the evening meal of curried goat and rice and breadfruit.

When the coffee arrived is when Sally began.

"Bill," Sally said, smiling and looking at him directly in the eyes, "Maggie tells me you have been coming on to her."

Farmer dropped his spoon on the floor and Edgar's mouth fell open as they all three studied the calm expression on Sally's smiling face. The only hint that she was not in a state of repose was in Sally's eyes. There was a glint of steely resolve in her piercing stare.

"What, what, what are you talking about?" Farmer was directing the question at Maggie, and his tone was aggressive.

"No, no, Bill, you and I are the ones doing the talking here for a few moments. Just consider Edgar and Maggie excluded from the conversation we're having now."

"Then what *are* you talking about, Sally?" responded Farmer, with a slightly more conciliatory tone in his voice.

"I'm talking about your sexually aggressive behavior toward Maggie, Bill. What you have been doing is inappropriate. You've been taking advantage of someone who is essentially in your care, and I think you'd better consider the consequences of your actions before this goes any further."

"What are you talking about? What has

this woman been telling you, Sally?" He looked and sounded like an innocent choirboy. Maggie felt uncomfortable watching him, because clearly his smooth professional skills would go a long way toward getting him trusted.

Sally did not budge, however.

"Bill, do not insult my intelligence by claiming no knowledge of what we're talking about. I know you have committed this offense, and you are in need of confessing your sin and seeking forgiveness."

As soon as he spoke, Maggie heard the haughtiness in his voice and, as he was speaking, Maggie could feel his unmasked hostility toward women.

"You have a nerve, Sally, accusing me of something I didn't do. But you also have a nerve," Farmer continued, "preaching the scriptures to me. It's very clear in the scriptures, in everything Paul wrote and in all he said, that women do not have an authoritative place in the preaching and teaching ministry of the church. Paul told women to keep silent in the church, and to leave the teaching and preaching to men."

Sally's eyes became even more focused on Farmer, like two search beams penetrating through him. She was not smiling now as she replied.

"Are you crazy, Bill? Paul was an old fashioned kind of guy who had a hard time understanding women — like most men I know — and you don't need to pattern yourself after his sexist comments. You're misinterpreting him, anyway. If you're talking about the First Letter of Paul to Timothy or about his statement in Corinthians, you know damned well how much times have changed since Paul wrote those words . . . if he did write them."

"I'm glad you know the scripture there, Sally," Farmer continued. "First Letter to the Corinthians, 14:34-35: 'The women should keep silent in the churches. For they are not permitted to speak, but should be subordinate, as even the law says.' "

"Paul was a good soldier and fellow missionary, Bill," Sally continued, "but I prefer to look to Jesus Christ to see the role women should have in the church. Jesus appeared first to *women* after his resurrection, and he told them to go tell the men that he had risen from the dead. All of the four gospels are consistent in that regard. He charged women *first* to tell the good news. Jesus was radical and inclusive in his treatment of women. And it is very clear that the Holy Spirit is calling women into ministry and into the pulpit to teach and preach. Why, fifty percent of divinity school students are women now. How dare you dispute the Holy Spirit's calling women into preaching and teaching? Don't forget Paul also says in I Timothy to not just drink water 'but use a little wine for the sake of your stomach and your frequent ailments.' You're a teetotaler, Bill. Why aren't you following the dictates of scripture here?"

"Sally, you know it's useless and vain to argue scripture, or to use it as a weapon to bully someone," Farmer replied.

Sally looked surprised. "I do know that, you're right, Bill. But I also know that I now see where you're coming from in your attitude toward women. You are a misogynist, Bill. You are a closet woman hater. And you are a sexual harasser."

"That is a lie! An outrageous lie!" He was thundering like a lion and was red in the face.

"What you have been doing to Maggie behind the scenes is wrong and repulsive, Bill," Sally continued. "You have been taking advantage of someone in a reprehensible way, and you need help with the aggression you feel toward her. But, whether you get help or not, I want you to know that I will speak up on behalf of this young woman if you continue pestering her. You may not be terribly impressed by the thought of two women standing together against you in your very male profession, but I just want you to know that Maggie will not be raising her voice alone, and she will not suffer in silence."

Sally paused, then continued again.

"If you make so much as one more move on this young woman, I'm going to know about it, and I'm going to rise to her defense. Furthermore, if you attempt to harm her career in any way, I'm going to be looking over your shoulder. You can put down women all you want to, but you know damned well that if I raise my voice to speak against you, my voice will be listened to and believed. If you cannot find your way to seek forgiveness and mercy so that you sin no more against this young woman, at least consider your own self interest. You do not want a long and distinguished career in ministry tarnished by the accusation of sexual discrimination."

He looked visibly shaken. His reddish flush had turned to a chalky, pale look.

"No, I do not want that to happen, because it is not true," he whined. "I am afraid Maggie has jumped to some rather serious and wrong conclusions."

"Just don't do it again, Bill. Do you understand?" She was glaring at him, clearly unsympathetic to his whimpering.

"If you'll excuse me, I'm going to retire now," Farmer announced. "The day has exhausted me, and I need the replenishment of sleep. Good night, everyone."

There was silence among Maggie, Sally, and Edgar after he left. Maggie guessed that Edgar's silence was the product of years of being married to this vibrant, vivacious, outgoing advocate. He had clearly been in this situation before in their marriage, with Sally passionately adopting a needy cause. He did not ask a question or propose a solution. He simply sat in silence, sipping his coffee and water, lending moral support by his silent presence.

After some silence Maggie spoke. "Thank you, Sally."

"You're welcome, dear. I think things will be better now. He knows it's not going to be a secret anymore, and people always like doing their bad things in the dark when no one can see them. Now that he knows that we know, he will behave more appropriately. We may not change his attitude toward women, Maggie, but we can change his behavior, I think."

Maggie slept better that night than she had slept in a long time. But with only two days left in Jamaica, she found herself so eager to hold her children and hug her husband!

Throughout the next two days it was as though the conversation between Bill Farmer and Sally O'Connell had not happened, except that Maggie felt somehow safer, at least temporarily. She had a champion and a protector as long as Sally O'Connell was nearby. Maggie wondered if there would be a backlash against her once the O'Connells were back in Japan and she and Farmer were back home. But she decided she wouldn't worry about a problem that hadn't happened yet and that might never happen. At least for now, she was being treated more like a dead carcass than live prey, and it felt more comfortable being ignored than hounded.

The day arrived for their departure home, and the O'Connells had offered to drive them to Montego Bay. Maggie was glad to be able to sit in the back seat of a car and simply talk with this woman whom she had come to regard as her guardian angel. The proverb, "How forceful are honest words," sprang to Maggie's mind when she thought of Sally. There was a holy boldness about this lady who nearly always had a smile on her face. Maggie so admired how Sally made no compromises with evil. Like the Old Testament prophets, Sally just stared evil and wrongdoing in the face and refused to let them be hid. Even Dr. Farmer had been silenced by this honest and outspoken saint. Only time would tell whether or not he was merely wearing a muzzle.

In the back seat of the car, Maggie and Sally admired the view of the ocean on their right during the two-and-a-half-hour trip. They talked of family mostly. Sally talked of her two adopted Japanese children who were having a hard time adjusting to American culture. For the first time in their lives, they were in a country where they looked physically different from everyone else, and they were not enjoying the experience of feeling like aliens. Maggie's thoughts kept turning to her own children. She was so excited that she would be home, sleeping in her own bed, very soon.

There were two cleanup crews struggling with the debris from Hilda in most of the more populated areas they passed through. At Discovery Bay — the place where Columbus is said to have discovered Jamaica — the beach was trashed with garbage and pineapple tree tops and wood of all shapes and sizes. "The land of wood and water," Jamaica was called, and the wood and water were mingled in a new way because of Hurricane Hilda. Uniformed Jamaicans did seem to be working busily in every town getting the island cleaned up and ready for its tourist business again.

At the Donald Sangster International Airport in Montego Bay, there was a whirlwind of activity. Apparently there were some chartered flights of tourists expected that afternoon, and there were people everywhere waiting to see a real live tourist again. Jamaica's major industry had been shut down in an instant by Hurricane Hilda, and now the tourism army of taxi drivers, car rental representatives, foreign exchange officials, restaurant workers, shop keepers, and miscellaneous street vendors was swarming the airport, eager to catch sight of skin that needed tanning, hair that needed braiding, and temperaments that needed soothing. To this laid-back Caribbean paradise, those tourists would be bringing the foreign currency that this island and its people desperately needed and depended on. It was a good feeling, Maggie thought, to be leaving the country just at the time when the tourist trade was starting to reappear.

Leaving the O'Connells behind at emigration was a sad occasion made easier because they would be coming to the U.S. in eight months and had promised to stay with Maggie and Kurt and the kids for a couple of nights while they traveled to various churches and visited their four children.

Once on the plane Maggie felt she was floating in a time capsule back to her loved ones. Ignoring her, Dr. Farmer busied himself with the preparation of a sermon that he was to deliver on Sunday, just two days away, and Maggie flipped from magazine to magazine in mounting anticipation of seeing her darlings.

When she and Dr. Farmer did finally arrive in Greenfield, Maggie had to restrain herself from running down the tunnel leading from the plane into the airport waiting room. As soon as she entered the waiting room, she saw Kurt! And the children!

"Jonathan! Look at you! You've grown a foot! And you, Ashley. You're even more beautiful than when I left! And Brent, you've gotten so tall while I've been gone." Maggie clung to them and they clung to her, like a Norman Rockwell picture of a mother with her three kids hanging on her like limbs.

Then she broke away and embraced her husband. It felt so good to be back in Kurt's arms.

At the end of their long embrace, Kurt looked at her with some obvious sadness in his eyes.

"I have some bad news for you, Maggie.

We got a call today. It seems that Laura is on her deathbed, and she's asking for you. She wants you to call her when you get home."

SAYING GOODBYE

By the time Maggie made the call, it was clear there was little time remaining until Laura's death. Maggie felt as though she were in a time machine. She had not had much time to be with the children and Kurt after she got off the plane. The children, especially the littlest one, had been so glad to see her, and they had clung to her and sat on her lap or next to her on the couch showing her the things they'd made and the grades they'd received in school while she'd been gone. They acted as though they didn't want to let her out of their sight. Mostly they had just seemed to want to touch her and be near her and feel the warmth of her presence. She felt rehabilitated and purified by their innocence and love.

Kurt seemed glad to see her but for different reasons. As usual, he seemed preoccupied with business. The homes he was building on "spec" were nearly finished with no serious potential buyers in sight. If three didn't sell within three months, his profit margin would be nearly eroded and he would be — they would be — in financial trouble, he told Maggie after the kids went to bed. But he was glad, he told Maggie, that at least her career was on a stable path.

The last thing Maggie did before taking a bath and getting ready for bed was call and make a reservation for an afternoon flight the next day. The airlines gave special prices to clergy flying to deliver a funeral service.

The children wouldn't understand why she had to go away again when she'd just gotten home, but at least Kurt understood that this funeral was very personal and very necessary. In fact, he told Maggie after she got off the phone, "Call back and reserve two tickets on the flight. I'm going with you. Mrs. Darcey can look after the kids by herself. Anyway, tomorrow is Friday, and she's already told me she can stay over on the weekend if we want her to."

Maggie and Kurt dropped the girls at school the next morning since their flight didn't leave until nine-thirty. They'd be in Chicago by noon and some of Laura's family would pick them up.

Actually it was Laura's husband, Jack, who was at the airport to greet them. He was alone. He grabbed Maggie and embraced her, and he kept holding her close for what seemed like minutes. Maggie felt like a life jacket being held by a drowning man. They did not speak about anything except trivia and technical matters related to luggage and baggage claim until they got into Jack's car.

"It's about a forty-minute drive to where we live, you guys," Jack said, as they rolled out of the airport and onto the busy freeway.

"How are you holding up, Jack?" Maggie was sitting in the front seat of the car with Jack, and Kurt was in the back reading the *Wall Street Journal* he'd bought in the airport. Jack sniffled and then pulled out a handkerchief and dabbed it at his eyes and nose before he began.

"I feel so miserable, Maggie," he began.

"I'm sure you do, Jack," Maggie said, trying to offer some comfort.

"No, it's not just that she's dying now. It's how I treated her throughout our marriage that's killing off a part of me, even as she's dying."

Kurt remained unobtrusive in the back seat as Maggie went about helping Jack deal with his grief. Kurt, like Edgar O'Connell, had learned the art of fading into the background that the spouses of clergy had to learn as a coping skill.

"Well, every marriage has problems, Jack. No marriage is perfect," Maggie offered, trying to be reassuring.

"No, I know what I did and how selfish and self-centered I was in our marriage. I can't blame anyone except myself, but my father was a real male chauvinist who felt that a woman's place was in the kitchen and bedroom. I didn't consciously adopt that pattern as a mold for myself, but all the memories flooding back show me that that's how I treated Laura."

Maggie decided just to let Jack ramble on and get his sorrow out in the open. Anger, bitterness, sorrow, and grief all mixed together as he spoke.

"Mostly I just wimped out on the relationship, Maggie. You know, Laura was more highly sexed than I am, and she used to beg me to come to bed when the kids were smaller. I never really listened to her or paid much attention to the emotional side of her. I just did whatever I felt like. Even when we did have sex, I was selfish and self-centered. It was when I wanted it, period. We used to go out on Friday nights when the girls were small. Sometimes we'd go dancing and then, as we got older, we just went out to dinner and to the movies. And we would often stop by my office on Friday nights so we could have sex. It was a quick five-minute exercise on the couch in my office. Very romantic, don't you think? Laura would do it cheerfully and without complaining, but I can see now how uncomfortable and demeaning and insensitive the whole thing was for her. She must have felt like a cheap prostitute getting through a trick. Oh, we never went home at the end of the evening to make love. We had dinner, the sex like I told you about, the movie, and then we'd go home and I'd turn on the television in the family room to watch sports while she went to bed. When we did have sex, that's the sex we had. My way, when I wanted, and however I decided we'd have it."

He paused momentarily to grab his handkerchief and dabbed his eyes as he choked back a sob. Then he recomposed himself and continued.

"Even when we went away, just the two of us, I did my own thing. It was my vacation, and therefore I was determined to relax however I wanted to. A lot of our trips were to New York and Boston and Maine to see friends. We would usually stay with *my* friends, and I would stay up late playing cards and talking business. There was seldom time for the sex and intimacy and companionship she wanted even when we went on vacation, because it didn't matter to me. She wanted romance and affection, but simply having her there was enough for me. It was just me, doing my thing and enjoying my friends, with her along for the ride. Take it or leave it."

He choked back sobs and then continued.

"I used to make light of her begging for sex or crying herself to sleep at night because she never got the intimacy she wanted. It wasn't just sex, I can see that now. It was intimacy she was craving, and I was the only man she could get the intimacy from if she was going to be true to her religious and moral beliefs. I guess deep down I knew she'd never run around on me, and she never did, of course. She was always loyal and faithful, like a dog. And that's how I treated her — like a dog. I can see that now, I can see all the insensitivities and emptiness and dissatisfactions and cruelties she had to bear. And there I was, on the face of it, a polite and caring husband who made a good living and took care of his wife and daughters in an exemplary fashion. I could have been 'Husband of the Year' to outsiders. But Laura bore her unmet longings with dignity, and I always knew I could depend on that. She eventually stopped begging like a dog for sex. And, although I didn't realize it while it was happening, she also stopped buying sexy nightgowns to attract me, and she stopped staying up late at night so that she could catch me awake and in the mood. She withdrew emotionally from me. We lived in the same house but we didn't have much physical contact anymore. We were actually physically separated although we were living in the same house carrying on a relationship that became pretty much all business. You know what I mean, family business, like who's going to pick up the girls from ballet and piano, and will you take me to the mechanic to drop off my car, and will you be here this afternoon when the plumber comes."

Tears began to roll down his cheeks.

"I see her dying physically now, Maggie, but I know she died emotionally about five years ago when I finally killed off the yearning she had to be close to me and the longing she had for intimacy. I can see now that sex wasn't all she wanted, although I denied her gratification there too. I brushed her needs aside as callously as I could. Oh, but to the outside world I looked like a model husband. I was a good provider, I didn't drink, I loved my children, and I was proud of my beautiful and talented wife. When she finally withdrew from me, I blamed everything on her. I didn't really think that any of it was my fault. I used to explode at her after the girls went to bed and call her every kind of insulting name, just to get back at her for being so cold. Deep down, I knew it was my fault, but

I wasn't going to take any responsibility."

Jack paused, then heaved a long sigh and kept talking.

"By the time we'd been married ten years, she had figured out how little she was going to get out of our marriage emotionally. And by the time we'd reached the ten-year mark, I was patting myself on the back for being such a good husband and providing an ungrateful wife with everything a woman could want. We weren't exactly rich, but I made nearly two hundred thousand dollars a year in the insurance business, and Laura didn't really have to work. She eventually ended up doing some substitute teaching after we put our baby in kindergarten but that was just to fill up her time. She didn't have to work."

He stopped talking. There was silence in the car for what seemed like minutes before he spoke again.

"I can see now that it must have been hard for her during the last five years. I mean, before she found out about the cancer. I think she really did stop wanting me in the same way. There was a sadness about her in the last few years. Oh, she never went to a doctor for anything like depression. She just began filling up her life with things — usually things she was doing for other people. She was involved in the Salvation Army love lunches and some church committees in addition to the substitute teaching. She was in the Junior League briefly but she got out when she found out that most of the women were a bunch of vain, pompous socialites full of their self importance. She never did have much use for hypocrites and fakes, Maggie, you know that. I used to resent all her involvements and activities. I felt like she was taking time from the family, and time from me. I wanted her at my beck and call, but I didn't want to really have to give anything in return, except the material things, which I thought she should have been very appreciative for."

Now tears streamed down his cheeks and he looked at Maggie quickly before turning his eyes back to the road. Then he spoke in a tone of voice that reeked of remorse.

"Do you have any idea what it's like to look at the woman you love on her deathbed, and know that you made her life a living hell in the area that meant the most to her? In the emotional part?" He sobbed and used his handkerchief on his eyes and nose.

"You know what an emotional and demonstrative person Laura was. People used to say she could have been an actress. She was a very physical person, and she kept herself in such good shape all the time. Until she recently lost all that weight, she was still a perfect size eight, maybe with a little flabbier tummy. All our friends used to be amazed at how sexy and trim she always looked, and I was proud of her for that, too. Of course I was proud of her," he said sarcastically. "She was my perfect trophy wife. I just never showed her the physical warmth and I never gave her the romance she needed. I didn't realize that, one day, she would just not want me in the same old way. She just checked out of the old 'Marriage Hotel,' in a way. Or I guess she just checked into a single room in the same hotel."

The car Jack was driving pulled into an affluent subdivision outside Chicago and, after winding along streets lined with large brick and stucco houses, it pulled into a driveway leading up to a three-car garage. The house had a large, elegant, and deep front yard which had a circle drive in front of the house where six or seven cars were parked. Jack pointed the electric door opener at the garage door and they drove inside the spacious garage which had room for two cars while also leaving space for a well-equipped wood-working area on one side.

As Maggie and Kurt made their way into the house, with Jack leading them to their guest bedroom upstairs, they passed by a bedroom with an open door through which she saw two girls. They were Laura's ten-year-old and fourteen-year-old daughters. Maggie had attended their baptism, and she had seen them from time to time through the years.

"Molly, Sally," Jack called to them as he stopped beside their room en route to the guest room, "you remember Mr. and Mrs. Dillitz, don't you? Maggie is here . . . to be with your mom." What Jack obviously meant to say was that Maggie was there to perform the funeral service of their mother, but those words were aborted in mid-sentence and replaced with other words. Maggie looked into the swollen eyes of those two young girls and suddenly felt like a jackal circling the not-yet-dead body of their mother, who was downstairs.

Momentarily, it seemed to Maggie that she was the Grim Reaper incarnate. Her very presence clearly announced that the funeral was certain and imminent. She felt like a burglar, and she hated her own presence in that house for a few dramatic seconds as she stood in the hallway simply staring at the girls. Finally, she managed a smile as she said, "Hi, girls. You've turned into real young ladies since the last time I saw you, and you certainly have your mother's good looks."

"Hi," was the subdued but polite response from the girls. There was a weightiness and sadness in their muffled voices that seemed inappropriate for the voices of children. But, then, it was inappropriate that their mother was dying downstairs.

Maggie could see from the guest bedroom that Jack had made more than a "good living" for his family. This was a beautifully designed home with a warm, southwestern decor that made Maggie feel right at home. The guest bedroom where she and Kurt would be staying even had its own bathroom.

"We wanted our master bedroom on the ground floor so that we could get old together in this house someday," Jack said wistfully, as he set two bags down on the thick carpet and then stared out the back window with his hands in his trouser pockets and his back to Maggie and Kurt. "But we decided to put this second master bedroom on the second floor in case we ever needed a mother-in-law suite and to give it better resale potential in the unlikely event that we ever sold it to a young couple with little kids who might not want to be downstairs. Oh," he sighed, "we never imagined we'd sell this house. It was our dream house. And I guess the girls and I will stay here after . . ." Then Jack broke into sobs. Maggie closed the door to the bedroom so that he could cry in private, without being overheard by his daughters, and then she and Kurt helped Jack into one of the lovely chairs near the bay window of this spacious, beautiful room. They stood on either side of him, each of them with a hand on his shoulder.

"You go on downstairs, Maggie. I know Laura wants to see you. Just leave me here with Kurt for a few minutes. I can't face the girls all broken up like this."

As she walked down the winding front staircase to the downstairs, Maggie admired the beautiful Mexican tiled floor in the foyer. At the bottom of the staircase, a uniformed nurse greeted her.

"Are you the lady minister?" she asked.

At the moment she heard those words, she caught the scent of an odor that smelled like medicine and decay. It was the scent of death. Maggie realized that, even if she were blindfolded, she could find her way to the room of the dying person in the house just by smell.

"I'll take you to Mrs. Youngston," said the nurse, looking very grim. Maggie pitied Laura for having to spend any of the final moments of her life with this grim-faced, unsmiling character. Especially Laura, who was known for her happy disposition and her ability to look on the bright side of everything, no matter what. Maggie made up her mind at that second that she was actually there more to help Laura die happily and peacefully than to conduct her funeral. A death with the least amount of horror and terror and fear was what Maggie would help Laura achieve.

When Maggie walked into the darkened bedroom with its luscious, thick, deep green carpet bordered by pale yellow walls, she realized what a happy and loving room this had been designed to be. It had never been Jack and Laura's intention that one of them would die, so young, in that room. Maggie walked up to the frail creature lying on the bed, hooked up to the intravenous solutions hanging from medical equipment near the bed, and kissed her on the forehead.

Like Sleeping Beauty, Laura's heavy eyelids opened halfway as she felt the kiss, and she rolled her eyes upwards. Her eyes crinkled in a smile, and the corners of her mouth turned upwards in pleasure when she saw Maggie.

"Maggie, Maggie, sit down, my darling Maggie," Laura said, gesturing her to the rocking chair near her bed with a skinny arm which had an intravenous tube running into it.

"Do you want me to open the miniblinds a bit and let the sunlight in?" Maggie asked.

"Oh, yes, please do, Maggie. This room is too dark, and I want you to fix me up. I want you to tweeze me and fix my face."

Maggie felt better when she adjusted the lovely yellow miniblinds to let the midday sun stream into the room. It had obviously been a room designed to receive the maximum amount of natural light. When Maggie walked back to the bed, she realized how young Laura looked. She was only fortyish anyway, but she looked like she was in her mid-twenties lying there on the bed. Laura had always had a perfect complexion, and the only makeup she'd ever worn was mascara and eyeliner to enhance her large, expressive green eyes. Those green eyes stared out now at Maggie as Laura said, "Maggie, I'm scruffy looking. Please get my tweezers and scissors out of the bathroom, and bring my eye makeup, too. I want you to tweeze my eyebrows and the hairs on my face to make me look like myself. There are so many indignities involved in dying, Maggie. I don't want to die looking ugly."

Maggie worked on Laura slowly and carefully for nearly a half hour, and Laura seemed to revive emotionally in the process. At one point, there was a knock on the open door of the bedroom and Jack called out, "OK to come in?"

"Just give us twenty more minutes. We're fixing ourselves up here," Maggie called back to Jack.

"Ahhh," Jack replied, "then I'll run up to the Fast Stop for some napkins. Be right back, honey."

After some plucking followed by the application of eyeliner, mascara, concealer, moisturizer, lipstick, and blush, Laura looked beautiful, although her eyes revealed the dulling influence of pain killers. Hair loss — not total, but extensive — was the price Laura had paid for her grueling and ultimately ineffective chemotherapy, so Maggie replaced the stylish head covering Laura was wearing with an even more chic leopard headpiece that Laura said Jack had just bought her the day before and which she had not worn. As soon as Maggie positioned it on Laura's head, Laura looked less like a woman leaving this world.

"Thank you, Maggie," Laura said, smiling as she stared at Maggie from the nearly upright position in which Maggie had placed her, lying back against the six or seven pillows propping her up.

"You're welcome, dear friend," Maggie replied, smiling back at this special, talented woman known for her loving nature and great intelligence.

"Maggie," Laura said, continuing to smile at her, "I want you to help Jack."

"What do you mean?"

"I mean, he has been such a good husband to me. He never had an affair, he was never disloyal to me in any way, and he really taught me how to trust people. But I never was satisfied all the way with our marriage, and I punished him emotionally for not meeting my every need. It seems so frivolous and trivial to me now, but that's exactly what I did. And I regret so much leaving him in some guilty state because he feels that he didn't quite measure up to my expectations. I don't want to leave him behind feeling guilty that he cheated me out of something or had something he never gave me. I loved him, Maggie, and I know he loved me too. Help him understand."

It was clearly a physical struggle for Laura to talk. She looked wilted just from that brief dialogue.

"Let me lay you back down," Maggie responded, lunging forward towards Laura as she listened to Laura's heavy breathing and saw how winded she was.

"No, no, I want to finish, Maggie, Jack will be here soon." She paused and breathed heavily and laid her head back briefly against the pillows as she caught her breath. Then she picked her head back up and looked into Maggie's eyes as she continued.

"If anyone has any guilt over our marriage, Maggie," Laura said flatly, "it should be me. I more or less gave up on our marriage at some point and I retreated into my shell where he couldn't reach me."

Now Laura's breathing became very heavy, and Maggie jumped up and repositioned her so that she was not propped up at such an angle but was lying in a flatter position with her eyes looking toward the beautiful, white, chandeliered ceiling.

"You can't withdraw from a marriage, Maggie. You can't let anything make you just give up. If I had to do it over again, I'd dig deep into my reservoir of patience and creativity and just put up with the ebbs and flows a little better. I hate to leave Jack with the feeling that he failed me. If anything, I let him down by making a unilateral decision that the marriage wasn't ever going to fulfill me. What that does is become a self-fulfilling prophecy. I gave up a lot of chances for happiness because I was too blind to see that we had all the important stuff . . . we just didn't have everything in perfect condition all the time. I love Jack so much. I just want him to know that. And, of course, my darling girls. I'm so glad they have a father like Jack. I'm glad they're as old as they are, too. I know they'll be alright. They'll be under the loving care of Jesus Christ." Then Maggie saw tears roll down her cheeks and heard a deep sound like a sob.

"I hate to leave my babies, Maggie . . ." The most mournful whimper Maggie had ever heard accompanied those words. Through swollen, wet eyes, Laura stared at Maggie and continued softly. "Life is a very brief adventure, Maggie. You can't trivialize it in any way."

As Maggie watched Laura cry gently at the thought of leaving her children, she observed the almost mystical breakthrough of Laura's characteristically sunny disposition. Maggie marveled as Laura's bright, positive outlook pushed through the melancholy and reigned supreme. There was a spirituality about Laura as she spoke next.

"Maggie, do you know what I feel confident about, though?" Laura was smiling at Maggie with such composure. But she looked more than composed. She looked clearly . . . happy. Happy?

"No, Laura, what do you feel confident about?"

"I do look back on my life with a few regrets, it's true. I mean, if I could do it all over, I would just love people more and judge them less. I would just spend my time loving and trying to love better. But I do look back at some parts of my life that now give me so much confidence. I am so glad I took my children to church. I am so glad Jack and I built a home in which we shared the Christian faith. If I hadn't planted those seeds of faith in the good times, Maggie, I don't know what I would have to harvest now. I do somehow have this feeling that I am in the middle of an abundant harvest now because those seeds of faith have grown and are nurturing me now."

Just then, Molly, Sally, Kurt, and Jack rapped on the door and burst into the room.

"Mom, you look gorgeous!" The girls were animated and smiling and their presence flooded the room with warmth and love. Sally laid down on the queen-size bed beside her mother, and Molly stood on the opposite side of the bed stroking her mother's cheek.

"You do look beautiful, honey," Jack said, smiling at her as he sat down on the side of the bed near Laura's knees. He took one of her small hands and held it gently between his two large ones.

Maggie felt Kurt's hands massaging her shoulders as she sat in the rocking chair with him standing up behind her. It was strange, but there was no feeling in this room that anyone was in danger. There was only a kind of calm assurance in the air.

This scene seemed so different from any other deathbed situation Maggie had ever seen. Usually her pastoral visits to a dying person would be performed in a hospital, where the patient would linger in an austere and impersonal setting, away from home, until death came. Maggie had often noticed that some hospital nurses didn't visit dying patients very frequently. It was as though they had the philosophy that "There's nothing we can do about the condition of the dying person; their fate is decided and nothing could be done that would make a difference." How different Laura seemed, dying in her own bedroom in as relaxed a way as possible, compared to those imprisoned in hospitals until released to the morgue by a death certificate.

As Maggie stood up to leave the room with Kurt so that Laura could have some privacy with her family, Laura motioned for her. Maggie bent down toward her friend's face, and Laura whispered in her ear: "Talk about love, Maggie, will you?" Maggie nodded, kissed her friend on the forehead, and left the room as she whispered back: "Yes, and I'll read you some love scriptures when I come back in a little while."

Outside Laura's bedroom the house was bustling with relatives and neighbors who had packed the kitchen with all kinds of food. Maggie and Kurt fixed themselves plates sampling the cold cuts, casseroles, and goodies and went into the beautiful sunroom at the back of the house to eat.

"I'm glad you came," Maggie said to Kurt, as they sat down on the elegant, multicolored paisley sofa to have their lunch.

"Me, too," said Kurt, smiling at her before starting to munch.

Maggie and Kurt decided to take a quick, brisk walk after lunch in the rolling hills of the affluent subdivision where Laura and Jack lived.

When they returned to the house twenty minutes or so later, they entered a house where they found crying and grieving the same friends who only moments before had been laughing and talking and playing board games in the family room. As soon as Maggie saw their grief, she headed for Laura's room with Kurt close behind. The nurse was standing over Laura, disconnecting the IV apparatus from Laura's arms while Jack and the girls stood near Laura's bed, huddled in a circle with their arms around each other.

"She left this world peacefully in every way, Maggie," Jack said quietly as Maggie and Kurt stood beside them looking down at the beautiful, lifeless body of the mother, wife, and friend whom they had cherished.

The next few hours were filled with the hustle-bustle of phoning people — relatives, friends, the funeral home, and church. Fortunately, some of Laura's friends from her church circle were there to handle the informational calls and to greet the traffic, so Maggie decided to steer Jack and Molly and Sally upstairs to the guest room where she and Kurt were staying. They responded mechanically to her suggestion that they go upstairs.

Once in the room, Maggie asked the girls to sit on the bed and asked Jack to sit in the rocking chair. Kurt sat in the chair facing the desk, near the window.

"I just want us to be in prayer briefly," Maggie told them. "Is there anything you want to ask God or say to God right now?"

"Why did my mother have to die so young?" Molly's response was immediate, and in her plaintive voice there was pain and sorrow.

"What is earth's loss, is heaven's gain," Jack said, in a tone of voice that revealed his inner strength as well as his deep sorrow. It was as though his voice was animated by something outside himself. His words came from the depths of his soul.

"I want to see my mommy again in heaven. She said I would," Sally spoke next. It was obvious that there was an air of unreality about all this for this little ten-year-old clone of Laura.

"Can we say a prayer together?" asked Maggie.

Father God,
Help us to cope with the loss of this beautiful woman
And loving mother and wife
By forcing ourselves to focus in these next few days
On all the goodness and kindness and lovingness
That she represented.
Etch into our hearts
The memories of her loving deeds and generous acts
And happy outlook on life.
May we mourn her in death as she would want us to —

With happy, smiling faces because we feel enveloped still
By the warmth of her love for us.
And may we be blessed by the kind of peace
That defies understanding.
Oh, Lord Jesus, when you left this earth,
You said that you would not leave us desolate.
You said that you would send us the Counselor,
The Holy Spirit,
To be with us after you ascended into Heaven.
We pray that your Holy Spirit and your mighty Counselor
Will be near us,
Keeping us secure in the knowledge that
Our darling Laura is with you in a heavenly place
Where we will be reunited with her one day.
Guide us as we make the next few days
A celebration of her life. Amen.

Every eye was springing a leak. The girls excused themselves to go to their room. Jack said he wanted to have a word with the senior minister of their church who was downstairs. Maggie and Kurt found themselves alone. Kurt closed the door, and they gravitated toward the bed and laid down together. Kurt wrapped his arms around her and Maggie snuggled near him.

"You're going to do a great job at this funeral, baby."

"I don't know about that, honey," Maggie said, suddenly feeling tired and weak. "But I'm so glad you came with me. You're keeping me strong so that I can be strong for Jack and the girls." They laid together and dozed off. Maggie felt safe and secure in his arms.

Downstairs, a few hours later, Maggie made some phone calls to the remaining Great Aldrich Eight. All of them said they'd be at the funeral on Monday. Maggie met many of Laura's friends and neighbors and, while making a kettle of tea, she met the minister from Laura and Jack's church.

"Oh, so *you're* the friend of Laura who wants to be involved in the funeral," was the minister's introductory greeting to Maggie as the kettle whistled. "I'm Dr. Monroe."

"Nice to meet you, sir," said Maggie, smiling and extending her hand. "Would you like some tea?"

"No, thank you. What I would really like, to tell you the truth, is to conduct Laura's funeral service," he answered rather abruptly.

Maggie stared at him, taken aback by the boldness and aggressiveness of his remark.

"Well, sir, it was Laura's wish that I do the

funeral service. I think you know that."

He stared at her without smiling and continued. "Now, I've talked with Jack in the last few hours and he doesn't mind how we do the funeral service. Frankly, the funeral service is more for the ones left behind than for the departed one, and this grieving community knows me and trusts me and, I might add, expects me to perform the funeral service. You're not anyone they know and it's going to be hard for them to accept comfort from someone who is a stranger . . . and who is a woman, on top of that."

"A woman?" Maggie suspected where he was coming from, but she wanted to hear him say it.

"Well, you know what I mean. Most people just feel that a man has the kind of broad shoulders that are needed in a funeral situation. Look, we both have the same motivation, I think — to help these people — but I think they will be far more willing to accept the help from me. I'm somebody they know and like, and I can give them the healing words they need to hear and will accept. You could assist me in the service, anyway. You could read a few scriptures."

"I'll tell you what," Maggie replied, irritated at his condescension, "why don't you preach the service that you're talking about on Sunday morning, at your regular worship service? That way, you'll be able to do the nurturing you're talking about."

He looked at her without smiling. "That's not the same thing," he answered.

"Dr. Monroe," Maggie continued, "I didn't come here to play politics over who is going to preach at Laura's funeral. She asked me if I would do her service, and I said I would, and *nothing* is going to make me not follow through on the promise I made to her. I'm not going to play games here, I'm just trying to do for a friend what I said I'd do."

"You women in the ministry are so determined to claim your rights that you just fail to see the reality of some situations. It may be just a cultural thing, but people expect to see men in charge of a funeral service."

"Well, sir," Maggie replied, taking the cup of tea and preparing to go into the living room to socialize, "people will not find a man in charge at this particular funeral service."

Duty and responsibility filled the next day and a half, and then came the appointed hour of the service. The church was packed to capacity and, in fact, people were standing outside every entrance to honor the sad departure from earthly life of this lovely woman who had touched so many lives in such loving ways. It was just ten minutes until the service was to begin. Maggie was adjusting her clothes in one of the Sunday school rooms on the second floor of the large church. Dr. Monroe had not offered his office to her, a normal professional courtesy extended to a visiting minister, so she had found the ladies' bathroom upstairs and then discovered an unlocked Sunday school room where she could read her notes, organize her thoughts, catch her breath, and say a prayer before leading this congregation in celebrating the life of a special woman.

As she emerged from the Sunday school room, the door opened into the path of Dr. Monroe who was himself apparently headed down the hallway toward the sanctuary. He eyed her coolly.

"Are you ready?" he said, in a frosty tone of voice.

"Not really, but I guess it's time," responded Maggie, trying to defrost his attitude by sounding friendly and nonthreatening.

"Well, I've been thinking about our conversation, and I have decided that I'm going to write a strong letter to your superior. You haven't demonstrated any understanding whatsoever of the kind of professional courtesies that must be exhibited in these kinds of sensitive situations. I intend to communicate in writing to whoever is your boss in order to inform him that I find you lacking in the kind of qualities that generally mark someone who is in ministry."

Maggie stopped walking and turned toward him to stare into his eyes.

"Are you serious? You're going to try to blast my career because you didn't get your way?"

"From what I hear, you've done an excellent job of blasting your own career," he said with a smirk.

"What do you mean by that?"

"Oh, I decided I would call to ask a few questions about you at Golgotha, and the first lady I spoke with — some volunteer on the phone — told me you have been on some funny kind of leave of absence that has something to do with an inappropriate sermon you gave."

Maggie continued staring at him boldly but she felt butterflies in her stomach. This service was going to be hard enough emotionally to preach without this guy getting her totally rattled mentally. He stared back at her and continued.

"Like I said, it seems like you've been doing a pretty good job of blasting your own career, doesn't it?" An ugly sneer was on his face. "Oh, look at the time! It's time for us to go into the sanctuary, my dear. I can hardly wait to hear what you have to say." With that, he ushered her through the hall and down some stairs and then up a few stairs to a side door that led into the sanctuary. They entered immediately, Maggie going first.

She tried to loosen up and release the tenseness she felt while the hymns were sung. Then she heard Dr. Monroe introducing her as a friend of Laura's who had been a classmate in graduate school.

Maggie walked up to the lectern and looked out at the sad faces of nearly a thousand people filling the large sanctuary.

"Before she died, Laura asked me to talk to you today about love. Those of you who loved her will understand that that was just like Laura — she was always planning ahead, and she even had a plan for her formal exit from this world. Although she had great admiration and affection for Dr. Monroe, I think she asked me to do the talking today because I have loved and cherished her through more than fifteen years of friendship."

"Laura didn't want to die. She especially didn't want to leave her children." Maggie could hear the muffled sobs in the audience.

"There is nothing sadder than the death of the human body. We know we're all going to die, but that doesn't seem to make it easier. We were created from dust, and to dust our human bodies will return, the scriptures tell us."

"But there is never a good time to die. There is never a best way to lose someone we love. We are never ready to let go of the human body."

"Death is, indeed, our darkest hour. We are in our most pathetic and most hopeless state when we are faced with the sting of death on our life."

"And we feel angry when we sorrow, don't we? We get so angry *at the power death has to break up homes, to take friends away, to chill the heart, and to make life dark and cold and lonely."*

"So what do we do? Well, we shed tears, don't we? Someone once said this about tears: 'Tears keep sorrow from becoming despair.' "

"If you are grieving over Laura's death, friends, then you will understand these mournful words of Lord Alfred Tennyson when he was sorrowing over the death of a loved one:

Oh for the touch of that vanished hand,
Oh for the sound of that voice that is still.

Oh for the touch of that vanished hand,
Oh for the sound of that voice that is still.

"Jesus had to suffer, too, because of human death. The scriptures say 'Jesus wept' when his best friend Lazarus died. Jesus wept because He saw two lonely sisters left behind, and he saw how death lords it over the living and governs us by anxiety and fear."

"In our darkest hour, when a loved one has died, we are so numb that we react coldly to almost any attempt to comfort us. We don't even much want to hear the 'good news' of Christianity preached to us in our darkest hour. Of what possible practical use can it be?"

"But there may be a morsel of comfort to be gained in knowing that the one who intercedes for us in heaven also tasted of the bitterest part of human existence. We know from the gospel story in Matthew that Jesus was terrified of death. Matthew says that Jesus was in agony in Gethsemane. He tried to pray in that garden, to relieve his fear, and try to make his peace with his impending death. Matthew says that after Jesus took Peter and James and John with him into Gethsemane, he began to feel sorrowful and troubled. Jesus actually said to his friends, 'My soul is very sorrowful; re-

main here, and watch with me.' "

"And then Jesus pleaded with God to release him from his ministry on earth. He prayed, 'My Father, if it is possible, take this cup from me; nevertheless, not as I will, but as thou wilt.' "

"Jesus did not want to die, any more than we want to die or want our loved ones to die. We have a Comforter who experienced the pain of losing friends to death, and of knowing he would die himself so that the scriptures would be fulfilled. It is that Comforter to whom we can turn in our darkest hour, because he knows what we are going through."

"And does he ever *know! He was spared nothing in the experience of death. In the gospel of Matthew it says that Jesus cried out just before his death, 'My God, my God, why have you forsaken me?' "*

"Jesus even had to face the responsibility of putting his house in order before he died, just like we do. The gospel of John says that when Jesus saw his mother near the cross, he made arrangements for his friend and disciple John to take care of her. He said to his mother, 'Woman, here is your son,' and he said to John, 'Here is your mother.' And the scriptures say that 'from that hour, the disciple took her to his own home.' "

"So it's a comfort to know that we have a saviour who understands the cruelty and anguish of death. He felt the cruel tentacles of death claiming him. He felt the terror of being stalked by the Grim Reaper."

"But the good news of that day of death called Good Friday was made clear after the miraculous resurrection of Jesus three days later."

"The gospel of John puts it like this: 'God so loved the world that he gave his only son, that whoever believes in him should not perish but have eternal life. For God sent his son into the world, not to condemn the world, but that the world might be saved through him.' "

"The gospel of John also records these words of Jesus: 'He who hears my words and believes Him who sent me, has eternal life . . . I am the resurrection and the life; he who believes in me, though he die, yet shall he live.' "

"Jesus said, 'Come to me, all who labor and are heavy laden, and I will give you rest. The son of man came not to be served but to serve, and to give his life as a ransom for many.' "

"Some of the most comforting words in the Bible are these, spoken by Jesus and recorded in John 14: 'Let not your hearts be troubled; believe in God, believe also in me. In

my Father's house are many rooms; if it were not so, would I have told you that I go to prepare a place for you? And when I go and prepare a place for you, I will come again and will take you to myself, that where I am you may be also. I will not leave you desolate.' "

"Listen to those words of comfort, my friends! 'I will not leave you desolate.' "

"Now if Jesus went ahead to prepare a place for us, then I think Laura is up there right now spring cleaning the place and putting flowers in it. I always think of heaven as an organized place, but with Laura up there, it's getting ready to get even better organized."

"Laura has gone on ahead of us, friends, to work right alongside our saviour, the saviour who conquered death. Death is not lord. Jesus is lord."

"Death is a sleep because of Jesus. The sleep of death is a holy and divine law to which everyone must resign himself. And we can find some comfort when our loved ones rest in the arms of Jesus, no longer touched by the world's troubles, no longer at the mercy of disease."

"Ah, but in our darkest hour, the good news sounds like such a bittersweet truth, doesn't it?"

"The fact is that the tenderest and most sincere sympathy cannot really comfort us when we are bereaved."

"But when we go to the Comforter in our grief, he can comfort us and he can tell us with authority that the prison doors of death will one day be opened and the prisoners set free."

"Laura was a Christian, and she knew that she would be received by a loving saviour after death. And that was a great comfort to her. She also took comfort in the fact that she had introduced her beloved children to the saviour, and that they would have a comforter and protector after her death."

"I marveled so much at Laura's wisdom during the last days of her life. I remember her telling me how important it was never to give up on love."

"I came to Laura's deathbed to comfort and counsel her but, instead, she comforted and counseled me. She was so wise in her advice to me to make sure to never let love get covered up by pain or hurt or by an inability to forgive a wrong."

"Love, Laura told me, is the very lifeblood of the human spirit and we can never permit that lifeblood to become tainted with coldness and bitterness and hostility and hate. Those things just clog up all our soul con-

nections and make us cold blooded."

"The Bible teaches that love is the key to a happy life. Indeed, this religion called Christianity teaches a very radical philosophy about love."

"Listen to how radical this is! We're expected to be Christian reformers in this world, but in a very radical way. Just think about it for a moment. Are we really expected to wage war with the pedophiles, and the murderers, and the pimps, and the rapists, and all those other 'lovelies' using **love** *as our main weapon?*

"Are we really expected to hate the sin, but love the sinner?

"**Love our enemy?** *Is this really the gospel message?"*

"Well, Laura asked me to tell you today that love is, indeed, the only thing that can influence or change human nature. Our man-made methods of judgement and punishment, necessary as they might be on occasion for our protection, don't change human nature at all. Only love can change a heart."

"The Apostle Paul in Romans put it like this. He said, 'You are circumcising the wrong thing! It's the tough foreskin of the heart that must be circumcised. Real circumcision,' said Paul, 'is a matter of the heart,

spiritual and not literal.' "

"Laura wanted me to remind you that love is the way to happiness in this human existence, and love is the key to eternal life."

"Paul was talking about love in Galatians when he called on each of us to be 'a Christ' to each other so that we can say, 'It is no longer I who lives but Christ in me.' "

"So let's rejoice a little as we remember and honor today this gracious Christian woman who herself planted so many seeds of love in this world. She believed strongly in the scriptural advice: 'Through love be servants of one another.' "

"We will miss this beautiful and gracious woman who loved so much and who followed the example of genuine servanthood as exemplified by Jesus Christ."

"Personally, I will miss Laura's wit and insight. She was the one I could always go to when I had a complex problem because I knew she could cut to the core of an issue better than anyone I ever knew. It was Laura I talked to first when I thought I was feeling the call to leave the business world and go into the ministry. I remember that she told me with great confidence that, if I prayed for guidance and for God's light, that I would know if it was genuinely His voice calling me. She was a wise woman,

and I respected her tremendously."

"Early in my ministry I was involved in counseling abused children who were hostile toward the concept of God the Father. As one teenager put it to me, 'If God is anything like my father, I don't want to have anything to do with him.' "

"I went to Laura for counsel and comfort and direction. She listened to me ramble on about my inability to reconcile the concepts of forgiveness and loving our enemy with the reality of young people being abused and mistreated and humiliated. I remember vividly how she just looked at me with a smile after I'd finished talking and said to me gently but matter-of-factly: 'Well, Jesus never said that being a Christian would be easy.' "

"In memory of this loving Christian woman, delight with me now in hearing again these words of Jesus about love from the book of John:

A new commandment
I give you,
That you love one another,
Even as I have loved you.
By this
All men will know
That you are my disciples,
If you have love for one another.

"Let us now close with this famous passage from Romans 13. Many of you know that this piece of scripture hung framed in Laura's home in a special place. I think these were her favorite words from the Bible:
If I speak in the tongues of men,
And of angels,
And have not love,
I am a noisy gong or a clanging cymbal.
And if I have prophetic powers,
And understand all mysteries and all knowledge,
And if I have all faith, So as to remove mountains,
But have not love,
I am nothing.
If I give away all I have, And if I deliver my body to be burned,
But have not love,
I gain nothing.
Love is patient and kind;
Love is not jealous or boastful;
It is not arrogant or rude.
Love does not insist on its own way; it is not irritable or resentful;
it does not rejoice at wrong; but rejoices in the right.
Love bears all things; believes all things; hopes all things;
endures all things.

Love never ends;
as for prophecies, they will pass away;
as for tongues, they will cease;
as for knowledge, it will pass away.
For knowledge is imperfect and our prophecy is imperfect;
but when the perfect comes, the imperfect will pass away.
When I was a child I spoke like a child,
I thought like a child; I reasoned like a child;
when I became a man, I gave up childish ways.
For now we see in a mirror dimly,
but then face to face.
Now I know in part;
then I shall understand fully,
even as I have been fully understood.
So faith, hope, and love, these abide;
but the greatest of these is love.

Back at home after the funeral, Maggie was told by Mrs. Darcey that Dr. Farmer had called and wanted her to return the call as soon as possible.

"Dr. Farmer?"

"Yes, Maggie," he said coolly. "Thank you for returning my call. We need to talk in my office to discuss the structure of your job. I'll need to report to the Administrative Board about the exact duties you'll be performing at the church, so we need to meet in person to iron out the details."

"Yes, Dr. Farmer, that would be fine."

"How about seven o'clock this evening?"

Why an evening meeting, Maggie wondered. Why couldn't he schedule their conference during the working day when his secretary and the office staff would be around?

"I'd rather meet during the day, Dr. Farmer."

"My schedule is very tight, Maggie," he replied angrily. "This is the only time I have available, and I am requesting your presence in my office so that we can go over matters pertaining to your employment here."

Oh, God, there seemed to be no way out. What was the right thing to do here?

"Alright, Dr. Farmer, I'll be there."

She had dinner with the kids and watched some of the news before she headed out, telling Mrs. Darcey that she had a meeting with Dr. Farmer and to tell Kurt where she was when he got home. She'd gotten an excited call from him that afternoon telling her that he thought he had a buyer for two of the houses. Pre-sale agreements had even been signed. He had sounded elated.

As she drove to the church, she felt tremendous anxiety about what was coming up. She didn't feel comfortable meeting with Dr. Farmer alone anywhere. Normally she had a sense of peace and security when she was on her way to the church. Sure, it was a place of intense work, but it was a protective sanctuary where she always felt safe. Except for now.

The church was locked, as she had expected it to be. She saw Farmer's car in the parking lot. As she put the key into the outside door lock and put her hand on the door handle to open it, she felt a sense of foreboding. Should she really be doing this? She sensed something that felt like fear and dread.

Almost instinctively, she pulled the door

back shut and locked it up tight again. She would not meet him tonight. She didn't feel comfortable doing it. At least, she'd drive around a few more minutes and think about it before she decided for sure what to do. She didn't want to be caught in another scene like in Jamaica.

She drove around town almost aimlessly for what must have been forty-five minutes, then returned home. She didn't communicate to anyone at home where she'd been or what had happened.

It was about one o'clock in the morning when she and Kurt were aroused by the sound of the front doorbell. Kurt got up and put his robe on and went to the front door.

On the front door steps were two uniformed police with a squad car standing outside in front of their house. At the sight of Kurt at the front door, one of the policemen flashed a badge in the sidelight window next to the door so that Kurt would have the confidence to know they were real law enforcement officers on official business.

"May I help you, gentlemen?" Kurt asked, opening the door.

"Sir, we would like to talk with Dr. Maggie Dillitz. Do you happen to know where she is?"

"Why," he answered in a surprised voice,

"that's my wife, and she's in the bedroom. We were asleep, officers. What's this all about?"

"Sir, we need to take your wife in for questioning related to the death of Dr. Bill Farmer."

"What?" Maggie had come out of the bedroom, dressed in her robe, and what she heard astounded her.

"M'am, are you Dr. Maggie Dillitz?"

"Yes, I am, officer."

"M'am, I'm Detective Sullivan and this is Detective Robbey. We need for you to get dressed, m'am, and come with us down to the police station. You're wanted for questioning in the murder of Dr. Bill Farmer."

"Murder?"

"Yes, m'am. Were you at the church this evening, Dr. Dillitz?"

"No."

"Dr. Dillitz, you were seen going into the church." He stared at her.

"Well, I mean, I was going to go into the church, and I did walk briefly into it, but then I decided not to go in."

The detectives and Kurt were looking at her incredulously.

"Dr. Dillitz, please get dressed, m'am. You need to come with us."

Maggie disappeared into the bedroom.

When she reappeared dressed in casual pants and a blouse, she turned to Kurt as the officers waited for her at the door.

"Kurt, I want you to make a call for me."

"OK," he said, staring at her with obvious confusion in his face. "What is this all about, Maggie?" he whispered.

"Kurt, get in touch with Mason Tribbles. Here's his card. Please call his New York office. They'll know where he is."

A look came over Kurt's face that could only be described as total shock. Not the jealous type, Kurt was an easygoing fellow who had been jealous of only one person in Maggie's past: Mason Tribbles. He knew Maggie had had a long relationship with this man who had been her first love, and he had always reacted with unmasked hostility when his name came up.

"Why Mason Tribbles? He's a criminal attorney, isn't he?"

"Yes, Kurt, he's a criminal attorney. And I think I might need one before this is all over. Please call him."

The employees of Thorndike Press hope you have enjoyed this Large Print book. All our Large Print titles are designed for easy reading, and all our books are made to last. Other Thorndike Press Large Print books are available at your library, through selected bookstores, or directly from us.

For information about titles, please call:

(800) 257-5157
To share your comments, please write:

Publisher
Thorndike Press
P.O. Box 159
Thorndike, Maine 04986